AMBERSTONE

MARGARET JAMES

AMBERSTONE

ST. MARTIN'S PRESS
NEW YORK

Library of Congress Cataloging in Publication Data

Bennetts, Pamela.
  Amberstone.

  I. Title.
PZ4.B4734Am 1980   [PR6052.E533]   823'.914   80-14017
ISBN 0-312-02156-9

Acknowledgements

As always, my gratitude to the following scholars and authors from whose fascinating works I was able to gain enough knowledge to write this book.

The Tarot	Brian Innes
The Twenty-two Keys of the Tarot	Arland Ussher
The Tarot	Alfred Douglas
The Tarot	S.L. MacGregor Mathers
Life Below Stairs	Frank E. Huggett
Mrs. Beeton's Book of Household Management	Isabella Beeton
The Victorian Home	Jenni Calder
The Best Circles	Leonore Davidoff
Crinolines and Crimping Irons	Christina Walkley & Vanda Foster
Nineteenth Century English Costume	C. Willett Cunnington & Phillis Cunnington
English Costume of the Nineteenth Century	James Laver

Prologue

The pond lay in a shadowed dell. It was very still, the reeds and grasses surrounding it decayed, as if Nature and the seasons of the year had forgotten them. Not far away the trees began. First, half-buried roots, twisting and snaking off in weird patterns; then, stout brown trunks, and finally the matted canopy of green, so thick that scarcely any sunlight penetrated to lighten the spot where the earth was scooped out like a deep saucer.

A lonely, lost place, tucked away between Balscote, Shutford, and Wroxton, in the northern part of Oxfordshire. Elsewhere in the district, wheat grew in rich, yellow abundance, and the hedgerows and meadows were powdered with wild flowers of every hue. But nothing grew in Devil's Dip except moss and fungi and the pallid fringe of vegetation round the water itself. There were no birds to sing, no butterflies to skim the air like flying petals.

The nearest village was Foxcove, but the people there had turned their backs on the Dip, pretending it didn't exist, for they were afraid of it, and what they believed lived beneath the scum-coated surface of the pool. The short-cut from Priddy's Farm to Foxcove, through the dell, was never used, men preferring the longer trek by way of Hanged Man's Path to get them home when their long day's work in the fields was done.

The big houses nearby ignored it too: Chorley Grange, Prince's Hall, Watermill and Amberstone. The gentlefolk had no reason to go there; the servants didn't dare. No one wanted to think about it; nobody ever went there, so it slumbered on by itself, waiting.

But one hot July afternoon in 1870, someone did come out of the woods and into the clearing, staring down for a long while, looking for a reflection which wasn't there. Too much slime and miserable water-lilies were in the way.

Time passed, but the silence was unbroken. The footsteps were not retraced to the sanity of Pope's Wood, and nothing moved. Yet forty minutes later, the hollow was deserted again: the intruder had vanished as if into thin air.

All that remained was a faded and patched apron, small in size, and a pair of black boots, scuffed, down at heel, with a hole in one of the soles.

It wasn't until the next morning that the farm labourers ventured into the clearing. They had searched everywhere else for Flo Piper's daughter, and this was all that was left. Their normally ruddy cheeks were pale, and they avoided each other's eye, talking rather too loudly to convince themselves, and their companions, that they weren't nervous.

When they saw the apron and boots, their pretence was over. No good fooling themselves any longer, and they picked up the shabby clothing and went back to Foxcove with heavy hearts.

There was no speculation, for everyone knew what had happened. For some mysterious reason, ten-year-old Minnie Piper had gone into Devil's Dip, despite the warning of her parents. She had gone in, but never returned. Whatever it was down there, under the lilies, had taken her, as it had taken others before.

Minnie Piper wouldn't be coming back.

One

" How very odd."

Lalage Ashmore was sitting up in bed, drinking her morning tea and reading her letters. Because she was young, lovely, and rich, she always had an abundance of correspondence; invitations to every conceivable social function, pleas for worthy causes, chatty notes from her women friends, and a reassuring quota of impassioned love-letters from susceptible young men.

" What's odd?"

Madge Commins, Lalage's maid, was mending a small tear in the frilled skirt of a ball gown, muttering to herself about the clumsiness of modern youth. She was round and comfortable, with curly grey hair and sharp blue eyes. She had cared for Lalage since the latter's birth. Now and then she scolded; many times she warned; occasionally she praised, but not very often, in case her mistress got a swollen head. But always she loved, with a deep tenderness and pride, hidden beneath a brisk, no-nonsense manner.

" I've had a letter from Rose Beeton."

" Oh, her! "

Madge sniffed. Lady Beeton was the dedicated gossip, with nothing in her head but the thought of clothes and jewellery, and other people's affairs. She was not Madge's type of woman.

" Yes, I know." Lalage smiled. She didn't like Rose much either, but then the slight frown returned. " But listen to this. She says: ' I had dinner with your cousin Prudence and her husband the other night. I was staying with the Felmans at Prince's Hall, and we all went over to Amberstone. Such a lovely place, I always think, although for my part I regard the peacocks as something of an affectation.' "

" Can't think why." Madge bridled. Any criticism of Lalage's relations was a criticism of Lalage herself. " Biggest peacock of the lot she is."

" Pea-hen. Do be quiet and pay attention." Lalage turned the page. " She writes in detail about what they had to eat and drink, and then . . . ah yes . . . here it is. She goes on: ' I must say, my dear, I thought Prue was really most peculiar, as if she were going off her head. She seemed so frightened too, and ill. I told Conan Kilmartin that his wife should see a doctor, but he looked right through me, as if I didn't exist.' "

" Good for him." Madge bit off the cotton with a snap and stuck the needle into the bodice of her morning dress. " That put her in her place."

" Maybe, but why should Prue be frightened, and if she is ill . . . ?"

" Probably all that stupid woman's imagination."

" But what if it wasn't?"

Madge shrugged.

" Don't like the sound of Mr. Kilmartin, I must confess, but I can't see him letting your cousin go short of medical care if she needs it. Why should he?"

" Why indeed?" Lalage was scanning the next page. " Frightened . . . Prue? What could be wrong?"

" Always one to exaggerate, is Rose Beeton. Take no notice." Madge surveyed her neat stitches with satisfaction. " There, that's better. Be more careful in future; this dress cost a lot of money."

" Yes, I will." Lalage wasn't listening, but an affirmative answer was always safest. " Should I write to Prue, or perhaps to Conan? I wish I'd been able to get to their wedding. It's so difficult to write to someone you've never met."

" If your cousin is going balmy, you'll get no sense out of her, and if Conan Kilmartin was brave enough to stare Lady Beeton out of countenance, he's bold enough to ignore your letter."

" What shall I do then?"

" Nothing. Mind your own business."

" It is my business, in a way. Prue's a relation."

" And Mr. Kilmartin's her husband. Let him look after her. Now, what are you going to wear today? The white silk? No, maybe the dark blue, as you're lunching with the Rossmores. More suitable, seeing they're only just out of mourning."

" I shall go and see her."

Madge turned from the wardrobe, lips compressed.

" Mrs. Kilmartin?"

" Yes. I don't like this."

" What excuse will you make? You haven't been invited."

" I don't need an invitation to call on a member of my own family. Give me my wrap please. I'm going to tell Aunt Ann."

Madge raised her eyes to heaven, but she knew her mistress's stubborn streak only too well, turning her attention to the fine cotton underwear, the elaborately constructed corset of figured satin with its firm busks, which Lalage's tiny waist hardly needed, and the shot-silk dress which would flow a treat over the small bustle at the rear.

At the top of the house there was a big room, filled with sunshine. The furniture had come from France, and was a delicate complement to the expensive carpet and light drapes at the window. Lalage nodded to Porter, her aunt's maid, just removing the breakfast tray, and then tip-toed over to the bed.

Lady Ann Burnett was very old. Once, she had been a famous beauty, but now, at eighty-five, all that was left were marvellous bones, and faded violet eyes in a face like yellowed parchment. She was really Lalage's aunt, once removed, on her mother's side, and although there was little hope that in her condition she would control the comings and goings of her great-niece, her very presence in the house was sufficient. Ann Burnett was an important personage, so well-connected that society smiled indulgently at Lalage's high spirits. After all, she was in Lady Burnett's care, so nothing much could go wrong.

" Did you sleep?" Lalage curled up at the end of the bed,

carefully avoiding the slight rise in the quilt where Ann's body lay helplessly locked with rheumatism. " You look tired."

" So will you at my age." Ann's voice was thin, but as ironic as it had been in the days when she was an acknowledged wit, with a tongue uncomfortably biting. " And what is wrong with you?"

" Does it shew?" Lalage never ceased to be amazed at Ann's percipience. " I thought I was hiding it rather well."

The bloodless lips moved fractionally.

" Not from me; you never do. Well, what's it all about?"

" I don't want to worry you."

" You won't. Nothing bothers me at my time of life. It's too late for fretting. Have you fallen in love?"

" Not recently." Lalage chuckled, then sobered quickly. " No, it's nothing like that. I've had a letter from Lady Beeton."

" An imbecile. Why Harry Beeton ever married her, I'll never know. What does she say?"

When Lalage had finished reading the relevant part of the note, Ann sighed, closing her eyes.

Lalage hesitated, wondering if Ann had dropped off as she did so often of late. Then she said tentatively:

" Should I go and see Prue?"

" Why not?"

" You don't think it would be interfering?"

" Of course it would be interfering, but you've already made up your mind, haven't you?"

" Witch!" Lalage took one of the tiny hands in hers. It felt like a few bones, lightly covered with dry paper. " I'm concerned about Prue."

" With some reason." The violet eyes opened again and met Lalage's squarely. " She should never have married Conan Kilmartin. A dangerous man."

" Dangerous? How dangerous?"

" Just dangerous, and as for Amberstone, that house of his. . . ."

" What about it?"

" Tales are told of it, you know. Strange, uneasy tales."

" Oh dear, you're making my flesh creep!" Lalage tried to shrug off her disquiet. " What kind of tales?"

" You'll find out soon enough when you get there. Take care, child, and don't go without Madge."

" No, but. . . ."

After a second or two, Lalage slid from the bed, very quietly, so that she did not disturb Ann. Of course, she was so aged that her mind wandered at times, and, as far as Lalage knew, her great-aunt had never seen Conan Kilmartin either.

" We'll go first thing to-morrow," she said to Madge when she got back to her own room. " Aunt Ann agrees."

She considered it prudent not to mention the strange, uneasy tales, for her maid was not in the least enthusiastic about the proposed visit.

" Send notes to cancel my engagements."

Lalage was contemplating herself in the glass by the window, only half her attention on the image thrown back. She was totally devoid of conceit, quite unaware that the deep russet hair, large hazel eyes, small straight nose and wonderfully-formed lips made her as great a beauty as Ann Burnett had ever been. She was wondering what her parents would make of the situation, but they had been dead for so long that she hardly remembered what they looked like.

" And when you've done that, you'd better start packing."

" I don't like it, and that's a fact."

Lalage picked up her gloves, drawing them on slowly.

" Neither do I, really, but it's got to be done. I must find out why Prue looks so ill, and, even more important, why she is frightened."

" That house, I'll be bound."

Lalage turned sharply.

" Amberstone? What do you mean?"

" Funny things said about it."

Lalage was wry. So much for sparing her companion from Aunt Ann's hints.

"What have you heard?"

Suddenly Madge became evasive, very busy picking up the discarded nightgown and wrap.

"Never you mind."

"Tell me at once! Really, you can be most exasperating!"

"Maybe so, but you won't like it."

"Tell me!"

Madge was still reluctant, shying away from the subject.

"Well?"

"Don't know much, in fact. Just what someone once said about there being a thing at Amberstone the family don't talk about. Only a silly rumour, I expect."

"A thing?"

Lalage felt a quick spurt of fear; a premonition of evil, which made her colour fade.

"That's it."

"You don't mean . . . a ghost? Oh, Madge!"

"No, I don't mean a ghost, and don't 'Oh Madge!' me. You'll wish you'd listened to me, just see if I'm not right. Whatever it is, it's been there a long time."

"You're talking absolute nonsense." Lalage threw off the tremor and said crossly: "I'm going now. Is the carriage ready?"

"It is." Madge opened the door. "Perhaps you'll change your mind after a night's sleep. My old gran always said never make up your mind until you've slept on it."

"Be assured I shan't change my mind." Lalage swept past in the most mistressy fashion she could muster, but she knew that the older woman wasn't in the least impressed. "We're going, and that's that."

But as she got into the brougham she was frowning again. Rose Beeton's letter had been disturbing enough; Aunt Ann's words even more so. And now Madge's comments had made it worse. A thing which had been at Amberstone for a long time?

In the late August heat, Lalage Ashmore shivered, but it was too late to back down now. She had burnt her boats. She would have to go to Oxfordshire to find out for herself why Prue, who had always seemed healthy enough, was ill. Even more important, she would have to discover why her cousin was so frightened.

Probably it was only the aftermath of childbirth, and nothing to do with the dark hints about the house near Foxcove.

She thrust aside her uncomfortable thoughts, and resigned herself to a dull hour or so with the grieving Rossmores.

To-morrow would be time enough to worry about Amberstone.

*　　*　　*

Just outside Foxcove, hard up against Pope's Wood, lay Amberstone. It was a jewel of a house, built in the late sixteenth century, surrounded by formal gardens, velvety lawns, statues, a fountain with cherubs at its base and, last but not least, a folly on the northern edge of its perimeter.

Inside, the graceful linen-fold panelling and old furniture, lovingly cared for, made it a place of peace, the sun glinting through mullioned windows, with bowls of roses here and there to scent the air.

There was not a sign of the demented clutter which fashionable Victorian houses boasted. No knick-knacks or footstools worked in hard bright wools; no bobbled, fringed and braided curtains; not a trace of sentimental photographs or coy china shepherdesses.

Just spaciousness and polished wooden floors, smelling of beeswax; air, light and total tranquillity.

It was nine o'clock, and silver chafing dishes had been placed on the sideboard in the breakfast-room. Mrs. Nuttall, the cook, had prepared the food: eggs, bacon, sausages, fish and chops. Frederick Crickett, butler of many years standing, had supervised the setting of the table, not trusting the maids to ensure that every piece of cutlery was in its correct position, and that there was ample marmalade, honey, and preserves to be had.

When Belinda Isard, the parlourmaid, put the coffee and hot milk in front of her mistress, Prudence Kilmartin murmured her thanks, praying that her shaking hands would not betray her as she filled her husband's cup.

Conan was deep in *The Times*, apparently oblivious to what she was doing, and she sighed in relief, grateful for a few more minutes in which to pull herself together.

She still could not understand what was happening to her. It was not just the sleepless nights, tossing and turning in bed, nor the frightening loss of weight which made the dainty sprigged muslin hang on her like a sack. There were other matters much more serious. She couldn't remember things, or where she had been. No recollection of what she had done the day before. Headaches were a permanent trial, the muzziness never leaving her. Underneath it all was the belief that someone had said something dreadful to her, but she couldn't recall what it was.

The servants looked at her strangely when she spoke, but what she had said slipped out of her mind before she could consider the words again. Whatever they were, they must have been stupid, for why else should the staff stare at her in that way.

She tried to tell herself it was because her son, Denzil, was only six months old. Women did suffer such things after childbirth, but the thought of Denzil simply brought a fresh wave of fear. She couldn't remember ever seeing him. After she had woken from an exhausted sleep, following long and painful labour, the infant had already gone. When she had asked for him, she was told he was in the nursery, being cared for by Mrs. Parkington, Conan's old nanny, and now his housekeeper.

She must rest, they said: she wasn't well enough to look after the boy.

Later on, other excuses were made; the nursery door was locked against her; her pleas to see her son ignored. There were occasions when she wondered whether he existed at all. Perhaps the child she thought she had carried for nine months, and which had torn her body apart, was merely another delusion. At other times, when she was more rational, she knew he was there, but her hysterical demands to go to him were met with a blank wall.

She was sure she was going out of her mind, and perhaps that was why Conan was determined not to let her near the son he had craved, in case she should injure his precious heir.

She stole a look at Conan, still reading the paper. Tall, spare, with thick, crisp hair and eyes like chips of slate. His nose was thrusting and bold, his cheekbones high, giving him an almost gaunt appearance. Always immaculate, always frigid, except in bed, and even there, there was no real warmth; just animal demands.

She hadn't wanted to marry him, frightened of him from the first moment her father, Ephraim Oldacre, had introduced them. In the beginning, she had no idea what was in Ephraim's mind. She knew that her father had squandered his fortune in gambling, and was near to penury, but she did not in any way connect this situation with the fact that Kilmartin had lost his wife tragically before she could give him a child.

It was only later she realised the two men were making a bargain, and that she was the pawn. Ephraim wanted money, and Kilmartin was rich. Conan wanted a young, healthy wife to bear his children, fanatical in his desire to have an heir to inherit Amberstone and his name. Oldacre might have been a reckless fool, but he came of a good family. Prudence was eighteen, and had never known a day's illness in her life.

When she saw Kilmartin eyeing her up and down, as if she were a brood mare he was proposing to purchase, she began to see what was in their minds, screaming inside at the very thought of it. She didn't know whether she hated her father more for selling her, or Conan for buying her, but, despite her youth, she put up a fight.

She held out as long as she could, but Ephraim was desperate, and when his shouts and curses didn't work, he used his whip. In the end, she had had to give in, going to the altar apathetically, her spirit broken.

Yet there was worse to come. She had led a sheltered life, and neither her widowed father, nor any of his female servants, had ever thought to tell her what was required of a wife. Her wedding night was an experience from which she never recovered. She had whimpered and begged to Conan on her knees, but it was useless. When he grew really angry, his patience entirely spent, he had simply stripped her naked and thrown her over the bed, taking her in what was nothing less than rape.

She shuddered, trying to put out of her mind the occasions of Conan's visits to her bedroom, which adjoined his own. But as she forced these thoughts away she found her gaze wandering round the room until her eyes alighted on the portrait of Conan's first wife, which hung above the mantelpiece.

Mercedes Kilmartin had been exquisite, with dark hair drawn back from a perfect oval face. The black eyes seemed to taunt; red, painted lips looked derisive. She was laughing at her successor, and perhaps at Conan too, for marrying such a frump.

" Why aren't you eating?"

Prue started, crimson flooding her wan cheeks, caught out because she had thought Conan's attention was elsewhere.

" I'm . . . I'm sorry. I'm not hungry."

" You will never get well if you starve yourself, and there is nothing more boring than a sick woman. What's the matter with you to-day?"

She tried to meet his cold stare, but couldn't, crushed by the sting of his tongue.

" Nothing."

"Don't lie." He was harsher still. "I suppose you had another nightmare." The lips thinned. "It is a miracle to me that, since you claim never to sleep, you still contrive to dream. For God's sake grow up, Prudence. Dreams are for children."

"It wasn't that."

She tried to defend herself, knowing that she was losing.

"Then what, pray?"

"I saw her again."

"Saw whom?" The dark eyebrows were ominous. "What on earth are you talking about?"

"I saw Mercedes, your wife. On the landing upstairs."

"You are my wife." The grating tone warned her of his mounting irritation. "Mercedes has been dead for more than two years. Don't let the servants hear you talk like that. They'll think you're mad."

"Perhaps I am." She was wilting, praying he would go away so that she could be by herself, yet, perversely, hoping he would stay a moment longer so that she could beg a favour of him. "Conan, may I see Denzil to-day? Oh, please say yes! I won't upset him, I promise, but I do want to see him. He is my son."

"Not whilst you are in this state." He folded the paper and stood up, adamant and uncaring about her tears. "When you know what you are doing and saying, we'll see. I will not put my son at risk."

She had known he wouldn't agree, but the pain was still acute.

"I think I'll go for a walk," she said finally, unable to bear the hostile silence any longer. "It will do me good."

"I doubt it, if you intend to go to the folly again. You know I don't like you seeing that disgusting old hag. How can you take her ridiculous Tarot cards seriously? If anything convinces me that you are no fit mother, it is this. The village wise woman!" He gave a curt laugh. "It is out of the dark ages, and she's preying on your superstitious credulity. What is more, she is trespassing. The folly is on my land, and she has no right to be there."

"She does no harm." Prue was pleading with him, hands gripped together. "Her hut in the woods is so small. She just likes to go to the tower now and then."

"Now and then! She's always there."

"I won't stay long, I promise. She does me good. Let me go."

He shrugged, losing interest as his eyes travelled slowly over her. Her blonde hair had been carefully dressed by her personal maid, Sabina Tuesday, not more than an hour ago, yet already it looked limp and uncared for. Her face was white as chalk, no blood in the lips. She saw his disgust and shrank back.

"Very well, damn you, go if you must, but you're a cretin to believe the tales she tells you. And for pity's sake tidy yourself up before luncheon; we have guests coming, and you look like a street walker."

She watched him go, tears unchecked now. She didn't love him, but his scorn hurt, and she knew he was right. She was a fool, yet she couldn't resist Nanny Peak with her rich, soothing voice, and the hope which the Tarot Trumps could bring. He was right about her appearance too; she was a sight. She would have to get back early, so that the sly-faced Sabina, with tresses the colour of a fox's brush, could help her change her gown. If she infuriated Conan any more, he wouldn't let her go to the folly again, and that she would not be able to endure.

As she crossed the hall, making for the garden, she heard Conan say bleakly:

"Yes. Mrs. Parkington, she's getting worse. Before long, I think we'll have to make arrangements to put her away. I see nothing else for it. There is only one place for the insane, and that is in an asylum."

*   *   *

Prudence had to shut her ears and mind to Conan's words. If

she had stopped to dwell on them, she knew her reason would really snap. There would be an explosion inside her, destroying her instantly. Besides, she might have misunderstood what he was saying. She was so often wrong these days.

She hurried over the lawn up a flight of stone steps, past an ancient sundial, and then along an overgrown path between high bushes. It was the only part of the gardens which shewed signs of neglect. That was because no one else ever went there, but she was glad to be screened from view by the hedges, even if some of the briars did reach out and catch at her skirts.

A moment or two later she was standing in front of the folly. High and stark, it was just like *The Ruined Tower* on one of Nanny Peak's Tarot Trumps. It had the same castellated crown, tipped sideways, as if it were about to fall, but never did. All that was missing were the tongues of fire, the bolt of lightning, and the two men falling from the top to the earth below.

Conan had said that the folly had been built by one of his ancestors, as a memorial to his eldest son, killed in a hunting accident, but he had never explained why the shrine had taken this form. Perhaps he didn't know. There was much about Amberstone which was mysterious.

The wooden door creaked as Prudence pushed it open. It was always a fearful moment, that first step or two inside, the damp and decay coming in waves to meet those who ventured in. There appeared to be no ceiling: one could stare up into endless darkness, just guessing what might be hovering overhead.

Then Prue gave a sigh of relief. There was a candle burning, which meant Nanny Peak was there, tucked away in a corner, with a flat stone in front of her which served as a table. No one ever saw her clearly. Prue hadn't, and she'd heard the servants whispering that they didn't know what she looked like either. All that people ever saw was a glimpse of mittened hands and the outline of a body, the head concealed by some kind of shawl.

"Well, my pretty, how are you to-day?" The voice was a deep whisper, but in the cavernous space it sounded like a weird echo. "Come a bit closer. No, no, not too close Yes, that's better. Well, what do you want this morning?"

Obediently, Prue stood on the spot indicated. From there, she could see the stone quite clearly, covered in what seemed to be a scarf or large kerchief of purple silk. Nanny always draped it with this before she laid out her cards.

"I'm . . . I'm not sure." Prudence felt a lump in her throat. The old lady was the only one who ever spoke a kind word to her, and it never ceased to make her eyes bright with unshed tears. "I'm no better. I still see things which aren't there; hear things which no one else hears. And they won't let me see my son. They say I'm mad, but I'm not, am I? Oh, I'm not . . . I'm not!"

"No, no, of course you're not, sweetling. Here, hold the cards. Shuffle them well; you know how."

Prue took the slim pack from hands which appeared to end at the wrist, for the rest of the arms were in shadow. It was uncanny, but by now Prue was growing used to it. She turned the Tarot cards as she had been shewn, some top to bottom, some the right way up. Then she gave them back, and watched the disembodied fingers begin to lay them out in a pattern on the bright silk.

They were beautifully made; each one a work of art. The wise woman had told her that they were a copy of the *Ancien Tarot de Marseilles*, and very valuable. She stared at each of them, willing them to help. First, *The Fool*, then *La Papesse*, then *The Emperor*. After that came *The Chariot*, *The Lovers*, followed by *The Wheel of Fortune*, *The Moon*, *The Hermit*, and others. Last, came *Death*, the most fearsome of the pack.

Prudence had found a book in the library about the Tarot cards, and had read it avidly. No one quite knew from whence they had come; all that was certain was that they were almost as old as time itself. She had learned how the particular pattern and lay-out of a group of cards could be interpreted, depending on the advice sought by the querent, and the juxtaposition of one card to those surrounding it.

Once she had tried to tell the wise woman how the cards should be read, and got a scolding for her pains.

"I've my own way of reading them," she had been told. "Never mind your book-learning, little miss. Leave it to me to tell you, my way."

"Ah yes." The forefinger stabbed at the card representing *The Lovers*. "A choice you have, that's for sure, but that choice is governed by its place next to *The Emperor*. A strong man, dearie. Powerful; a ruler."

"Like my husband?"

"Maybe. Let's see what's next. Yes, there's *The Woman Pope*, full of hidden knowledge. Won't get it by asking: comes with intuition. And here's *The Chariot*, triumphant, but crushing everything in its path. Good thing it's next to *The Wheel of Fortune*. That means change, but is it good or bad? Never the same, of course. Round it goes, up and down. Happiness and despair; never stays still."

"But what does it mean for me? How does it help?"

Prudence's voice was high-pitched, impatient for the final counsel.

"Well, it's hard to say."

The hands were withdrawn, only the pictures remaining visible.

"Some would say one thing, some another, but my interpretation is this. There's a person near you who would harm you, but another who would help, if asked. Much confusion and dismay, and that which you would see, you never will."

"My son!" Prue was stunned. "You don't mean my son? Are you saying that I shall never see him? Never?"

"Not I: the cards. But we'll have to see to-morrow. Come again, same time. We'll try once more."

"Yes, yes, I will, but please, please don't say I won't see Denzil. Oh, please don't!"

"To-morrow. Go now."

" My head aches. I can't think."

" I know, I see it here. Put half a sovereign down by your feet."

Prue always carried a few coins when she visited Nanny Peak. Her help had to be paid for.

" Good, good. Now, as you leave, look to the right of you. On a small ledge you'll see a phial. Drink it up, and you'll be better. Drink it all; every drop."

Prue turned away, blinded by sorrow, her heart heavy. Never to see Denzil. It was unbearable, but there was always hope. Perhaps to-morrow the cards would fall differently, and she would be shewn a way whereby she could see the child she longed for.

The phial was where Nanny Peak had said it would be, and Prue drank its contents, completely trusting. As she turned back to say good-bye the candle had gone out, and the tower was in darkness. She knew that if she called out, there would be no answer. Nanny Peak had gone.

When she reached her bedroom, she began to feel faint. The headache was worse, and the world was swimming round her until she felt she must surely fall from it and whirl out into space.

She lay on the bed, praying that no one would come. It couldn't be time to dress for luncheon yet; it would be another half hour or more before Sabina Tuesday arrived to make her mistress presentable.

Prue closed her eyes, but the giddiness remained. Then, quite suddenly, everything was still, and she sat bolt upright. All at once she knew what she had to do. She must go to the nursery on the third floor and demand to see Denzil. Whatever Nanny Peak had given her in the draught had produced the determination and strength which she required.

She ran up the stairs, meeting no one. On the second floor, at one end of the corridor, there was a carved screen, and behind it a lovers' seat. Prue had often wondered how many daughters of the house had crept past that screen at night to hold hands with their beloved. She didn't stop to ask herself how the lovers had gained entry to a house so well protected with locks and bolts as Amberstone; that would have spoiled the romance. She preferred to think of the gentle touch of one hand on another, lips meeting lips in ecstasy. So different from Conan, who had no hint of softness in him, and whose grip on her arms left bruises. When he kissed her, he was savage, as if he hated her, and once he was done with her, he always left without a word.

Up one more flight to the nursery floor, the long-dead lovers drowned in Conan's brutality, tapping on the door with tentative fingers. When nothing happened, she knocked more loudly, and then hammered as hard as she could, crying out and demanding entry.

Finally the door opened, and there was Mrs. Parkington. She wore black fustian, and a white apron, with a leather belt from which a bunch of keys jangled. Her hair was scanty, drawn back from a bony face in which light blue eyes stared in hostility at the intruder.

"Madam?"

"Let me in!" Prudence tried to thrust past the woman, but Mrs. Parkington's hand was like iron. "Let me in! I want to see my son. You have no right to stop me. You are a servant, and I'm the child's mother. Get out of my way! Let me go!"

"Now, now." Prudence was forced backwards into the corridor. "We mustn't get excited, must we? Master wouldn't like it, you know that."

"I don't care what he would like. I want to see my baby."

"Oh, I think you do care." The housekeeper was firm. "Master can be fearsome when he's angered. You know that don't you."

Prudence hesitated. It was a threat, and even in her frenzy she recognised it. Mrs. Parkington's message was unspoken but clear. If she, Prudence, did not go away and stop her hysteria, Conan would be called. And the woman was right; Conan in a rage could be cruel.

"I . . . I . . . just wanted a peep," said Prudence lamely, the fight gone out of her. "I wouldn't touch him, I promise. Just one look."

"I don't think so." Mrs. Parkington was triumphant, beginning to close the door. "Mr. Conan wouldn't like it. Besides, madam, you remember what happened last time you saw Master Denzil, don't you? Mustn't have a repetition of that, must we?"

The door shut tight in Prudence's face, and she turned away. What took place last time? She couldn't remember anything happening. She couldn't even remember seeing Denzil; not ever.

Slowly she went back to her room, shoulders slumped in defeat. Sabina was there, waiting for her, taking in every detail, weighing and assessing the shortcomings.

"Better get changed, m'm," said Sabina finally, pointing to the bed where a dainty blue gown lay ready. "Only half an hour before master's guests due. Don't want them to see you like this, do we?"

She drew Prudence to the long mirror by the window, holding her there, fox-face peeping over her shoulder, forcing her to see the wisps of hair, the smudge on the forehead, the torn dress, the tear-stained cheeks.

Prue cringed.

"Very well. Help me."

"Of course. Here, let's get that rag off first. Where you been?"

"To the folly."

"Oh yes." Crafty eyes met hers. "Saw Nanny, did you?"

"Yes."

"Shrewd one, she is. Gave her a bit, I hope."

"Yes, I always do."

"That's best. Don't do to offend."

The hair was released from its pins, the girl brushing away vigorously.

"Thought I heard you upstairs just now."

Prue sat stiffly in front of the dressing-table, refusing to bend to the inquisition. She hated her maid from the tip of her tawny head to the small feet, which could move so soundlessly along the passages. Conan refused to get rid of her, saying Prudence was being fractious again, but he didn't have to put up with Sabina.

"Yes, I was sure I did." Sabina was unsquashable. "Shouldn't go up there. Too risky."

Prudence turned quickly, her irritation, and determination not to discuss her private affairs with a servant, forgotten.

"Risky? What do you mean? How could visiting my son be risky?"

"Ah, but you didn't visit him, did you?" The smile was secretive and gloating, expert fingers at work. "Didn't let you in, did she? Don't blame her, really. When you saw the poor little soul before, they stopped you. Next time, they mightn't be so lucky."

"I don't understand."

Prue sat frozen, looking at a stranger in the mirror. A face delicately powdered and rouged, a mouth artificially red. Her hair was pulled so tightly back that it seemed to drag at the temples before the well-ordered curls began.

"No, don't suppose you do, seeing you are as you are."

The grin was only partly-concealed, and Prue knew that she was meant to see it.

"What . . . what happened . . . last time?"

"Best go down now" Sabina's work was done, and she was on her way. "Master'll blame me if you're late."

"Tell me! What did I do?"

"Nothing." Bleached lashes concealed the maid's expression. "Nothing at all. Got to you before you could do ought. But, like I says, they mightn't always be so lucky."

The starched frock swished through the door, the gap closing.

"Best leave him be. Next time you might really do it."

Two

Lalage arrived at Amberstone at five o'clock on the following afternoon. Had her sense of disquiet not increased since the receipt of Lady Beeton's letter, she would have enjoyed the peace of the Oxfordshire lanes and bye-ways, for the county wore its late summer garment with flaunting pride. So many wild flowers which Lalage didn't recognise, and trees, bushes and shrubs, each with their own lush tint of green.

When the carriage stopped in the drive, Lalage felt the oddest sensation catch at her. She couldn't define it, but it had nothing to do with her fears for Prue. Slowly she got out, looking about her.

"Madge."

"Mm?"

Madge straightened her bonnet, preparing to deal with the luggage.

"It's a fine house, isn't it? I hadn't realised it was so old."

"Aye, it's old right enough, and that's not all that's wrong with it either. Ah, good, someone's coming at last. Thought they were going to leave us standing here all night."

"Madge."

"What now?"

"Do you believe in reincarnation?"

"Good heavens no! What a question! What made you think of that?"

Lalage was uncertain; not her usual decisive self.

"I'm not sure. It's just that . . . well . . . I seem to know this place. In fact, I'm sure I do. I've been here before."

" What twaddle! You've never set foot in Oxfordshire, never mind Amberstone."

There was no more time for argument, for a thin man with small, shifty eyes had come forward, followed by a sturdy youth, and a maid in neat print and apron.

" I'm Crickett, madam," he said smoothly. " Mr. Kilmartin's butler." His gaze slid momentarily to the boxes which Madge and the coachman had deposited on the drive. " Is the master expecting you?"

" I doubt it." Lalage had shrugged off whatever it was that had perplexed her a moment or two before. Madge was right: she'd never been in this part of the country in her life. " I'm Lalage Ashmore, Mrs. Kilmartin's cousin. Be so good as to arrange for my trunks to be taken into the house."

Crickett cleared his throat, whilst the lad and maid waited motionless for his orders. Before he could either obey, or object to, Lalage's peremptory instructions, the sound of a horse could be heard, growing louder by the second until finally the sweating bay was brought to a stop not three feet from where Lalage was standing.

She knew at once who he was. Not only because Aunt Ann had warned her that Conan Kilmartin was dangerous, and this man, under the excellence of his riding habit, had muscles like steel, and eyes colder than any she had seen before. There was more to it than that. It was the same queer feeling that she had had about the house itself: a certainty that she had known him at some time in the past. Known him, and known him well.

For a split second she thought she saw recognition in him. Then it was gone, and it was he who spoke first, for Lalage seemed to have lost her tongue.

" Well, who are you, and what do you want?"

It wasn't an encouraging beginning, but there was no question of turning tail and getting back into the carriage again. She forced absurd thoughts out of her mind, matching her tone to his.

"I'm Lalage Ashmore, Prue's cousin."

"That answers the first part of my question." He gave her no quarter. "And what of the second part?"

"I want to see Prue." Lalage knew that if she shewed the slightest sign of nervousness now, she would be sent packing forthwith. "I have had a most disturbing letter about her from Rose Beeton, and have come to see for myself what is wrong."

"Have you indeed? How kind."

"Not really." She wished he would get off his horse, for she felt like a small insect he was about to step on. "She is my cousin, after all, and it is my duty. I trust you have no objection to my visit."

The gauntlet was thrown down, but Kilmartin didn't pick it up. Instead, he gave a brief shake of his head, snapped his fingers at the butler, and dismounted in one swift, lithe movement.

"No. Crickett, we'll have tea in the sitting-room, and tell Mrs. Parkington to prepare a room for Miss Ashmore and her . . . chaperone."

"Madge Commins is my maid," said Lalage tartly. "I did not think I would need a chaperone in Prue's home."

"Let us hope that you are right. Come."

He walked into the house without even waiting to see if she were following, and she gritted her teeth. It was not going to be easy. Dangerous Conan might be; rude he certainly was.

"Sit down." He indicated a sofa, taking up a position by the fireplace, as if to assess in greater detail his unexpected, and clearly unwelcome, guest. "You must be tired after your journey."

"Not at all. It is good of you to let me stay. I really should have written first."

"Yes, you should."

She looked up, startled by his bluntness, and it was then that the unaccountable feeling caught at her in earnest. She still didn't understand it. Not exactly fear, and not quite attraction. More a sense of knowing or belonging.

" I'm sorry."

She got the apology out at last, but he waved a dismissive hand.

" Never mind, you're here now. And what did that tittle-tattling woman have to say about my wife?"

Lalage moistened her lips, choosing her words with care, aware that since they had entered the room, Conan had not taken his eyes off her.

" Well, she said Prue looked ill, and was most . . most . . ."

" Most what?"

" It's hard to explain."

" But I'm sure you'll manage it." He was suave, and she knew that he was laughing at her. " What else?"

" That she was strange. Most peculiar, Rose said."

The lips tightened, and if there had been any humour in him before, it was gone now.

"In a way she's right, foolish though she is. Prudence hasn't been herself since the child was born. It does happen, you know."

" Yes, of course, but . . ."

Lalage turned as the door opened, expecting to see the parlourmaid with the tea. Instead, a girl stood there whom she scarcely recognised. Her fair hair was untidy and dull, her dress stained, her body wasted. Lalage got up slowly, not believing it, yet forced to accept the truth.

" Prue? Dearest Prue, you look. . . ."

She couldn't say it, although she wanted to cry out and demand what had happened to the apple-pink cheeks, the round, supple limbs, the gay blue eyes, and neat, smooth hair the colour of corn.

Prue wasn't paying attention to Lalage. She was more concerned by her husband's presence, like a rabbit transfixed by a snake which was about to devour it. Kilmartin gave her a brief, disinterested glance, and said tonelessly:

" Sit down, Prudence, tea is coming. I'm sure you've got

much to say to your cousin. It is thoughtful of her to visit us, isn't it?"

Lalage ignored the sarcasm which was meant for her.

" My dear." She turned resolutely back to Prue. " Yes, do come and sit down here, next to me. You look so poorly. Whatever is wrong? And how is your baby?"

Prudence whimpered and began to back away.

" Prue!" Lalage was shocked. It was like watching an animal which expected to be beaten. " Sweetest, don't . . . don't . . . Come here by me, and tell me all about your lovely Denzil."

Prue gave one muffled, hopeless cry and fled, leaving Lalage standing in the middle of the room, feeling a fool. She was spared the worst of her embarrassment, for Belinda Isard came in with a tray, followed by a young girl who placed the cake-stand by the side of the chesterfield, bobbing nervously to Kilmartin.

" Thank you, Isard: Worboys. That is all."

He waited until they had gone, then looked back at Lalage.

" It seems you will have to pour. I apologise for my wife, but, as you see, she is not herself."

" But what's wrong with her? I hardly knew her. She has lost so much weight, and seems . . ."

" Peculiar? Isn't that what the Beeton woman said?" Kilmartin abandoned the fireplace and sat down opposite Lalage. " She was right. Since Denzil's birth, Prudence has got steadily worse, both physically and mentally."

" But why? What does the doctor say?" Lalage did her best to keep her hands steady on the silver teapot. " Can't he do anything?"

" He gives her tonics, of course, but they don't seem to help. Time will heal her, so he says. She won't see the child. She hasn't seen him since the day he was born."

" What!"

Lalage almost dropped the cup, and Conan leaned forward to take it from her.

" But who looks after him?" Lalage was glad to take a sip of her own tea, for she needed something to steady her. " I don't understand. Why won't she see him?"

" We don't know why, and as to who cares for the boy, that is Mrs. Parkington, the housekeeper. She spends most of her time with him. There are plenty of other servants to deal with the running of the house, and we have daily help from the village too. Denzil is perfectly all right."

" May I see him?"

A veil was drawn over Conan's eyes, and he said softly:

" I think not. Only Mrs. Parkington and I see him. It's safer that way."

" Safer?" Lalage put her cup down hastily. " What on earth do you mean, Conan? Are you saying the boy is in some kind of danger?"

He avoided her question, simply shaking his head and repeating his previous assurance.

" He is all right."

" But surely you're not going to leave things as they are? You can't just sit back and do nothing to help Prue. There must be other doctors. Get a second opinion."

" I have the greatest faith in Dr. Morefield, and you may be assured that I am quite capable of caring for my own wife. Time is what is needed, as I have told you."

It was a slap across the face, but it merely stiffened Lalage's determination.

" Well, I think it is wrong. I don't believe time alone will help. She needs more than that. It is most unnatural for a mother not to want to see her child."

" You are an authority on such matters?"

Now the voice was as chilly as the eyes, and some of the heat went out of Lalage's indignation.

" Well, no, but . . ."

" Then I suggest that you leave the problem to those who are. Some cake? We have a very good cook. Such a pity Prudence doesn't take advantage of it, but perhaps you'll be

B

able to persuade her to eat during the next day or two you are here."

A time-limit set on her stay, and a high wall erected as far as the care of Prue was concerned. Lalage abandoned the head-on confrontation, and said lightly:

" Yes, perhaps I will."

The silence was heavy, Lalage crumbling a slice of Madeira which she didn't want, her cheeks warmer than usual. She was trying to think of some harmless topic of conversation, when she caught sight of a portrait over the mantlepiece.

" My first wife, Mercedes." Kilmartin was lighting a cigar. " I hope this doesn't bother you."

" No, no, of course not. Yes, I'd heard that she had died in sad circumstances. I'm so sorry. She was very beautiful."

" Yes, and strong too. There was no weakness in her, none at all."

The comparison with Prudence was too pointed to be mis-understood, but Lalage did not rise.

" Not all women are made the same."

" Thankfully, no."

She would like to have gone back to the subject of Prue, even if it had meant another snubbing, but he had got up, forcing her to do the same. Clearly, the interview was over.

He pulled the bell-cord by the hearth, and then walked over to her. She could feel an extraordinary quickening of her heart-beat, and it was as much as she could do to raise her head to meet his gaze. She wanted to turn away, to escape from the unexpected effect he was having on her, but she knew she couldn't. She was not going to let Kilmartin think she was weak too.

" I hope you will find your room comfortable," he said finally, breaking what seemed to Lalage to be an interminable pause. " If there is anything you need, you have only to ask for it. We dine at eight-thirty, and, meanwhile, welcome to Amberstone, if only for a short time."

She nodded, somehow depressed by the reminder that her

stay was to be so brief. It wasn't the thought of leaving Prue which saddened her, but another reason which she refused to dwell on.

" And now, I fear that I have been remiss. It is not often that one has the chance of welcoming a kissing cousin, and I ought to make the most of it."

Before she could move, he had bent his head and kissed her full on the mouth, one hand on her cheek. She was stunned, for it was the very last thing she had expected, but under the surprise there was the same sense of déja-vu. Tantalizingly elusive; gone too quickly to grasp at. Just a wisp of memory, disappearing as swiftly as it had come.

When his hand dropped to his side, she pulled herself together. Certainly it had not been a cousinly salute, but it was impossible that he had kissed her like that before; equally absurd that she had responded to him.

" Ah, Crickett, there you are. Is Mrs. Parkington ready?"

Lalage forced herself to pay attention, and if the butler had noticed her confusion, he gave no sign of it as he led her from the room.

Conan considered the burning end of his cigar reflectively: then he looked up at the portrait of Mercedes.

"Delightful, isn't she? Lovelier than you, I think, my dear. You won't frighten her, as you frighten Prudence. She'll put up a fight: she always had courage. Do you know, I think I am going to enjoy the next two days."

*　　　*　　　*

Madge was adding the last touches to Lalage's toilet. Light yellow gown, with faille underskirt of deeper colour; smooth satin hitched over the bustle, falling down in a myriad of ruffles to a small train. The bodice was cut low, shewing Lalage's creamy shoulders and neck, a delicate froth of lace hiding the curve of her breasts. She wore pearls, a touch of powder, with fragrant perfume behind her ears. For some obscure reason, she felt she must look her best that night, urging Madge to take care with the dressing of her hair until the latter said exasperatedly:

"Really! Anyone 'ud think you were going to Court, instead of dining with relations in the country. What a to-do about nothing, and your hair's perfectly all right."

Lalage ignored the crossness, meeting Madge's eyes in the mirror.

"Have you seen her yet? Prue, I mean."

"No, not yet, but I've heard plenty about her from those magpies downstairs, I can tell you."

Lalage was stroking her fan, trying to sound as if she didn't care.

"What sort of things?"

"Well, it seems the birth of the bairn turned her head. She's going out of her mind, so they say. Lady Beeton was right for once. And another thing."

Lalage tensed.

"They say she tried to harm the child; wanted to kill it as soon as it was born."

Lalage turned cold. She was remembering what Conan had said. Only he and Mrs. Parkington ever saw Denzil: it was safer that way.

"I don't believe it."

She defended Prue quickly, more because of her own dread than for any other reason.

"Well, maybe you don't, but that's what they all say. Terrible night, it was, according to cook. Screams and shouts, and Mrs. Kilmartin like a wild animal. Horrible!"

"It's not true! It can't be!"

"She seems normal to you then?"

The ugly truth forced Lalage to abandon her championship.

"No, not exactly. She seems ill and strange."

"There you are then." Madge was satisfied, her point driven home. "They're right, that lot below stairs. She is going mad, poor lamb. So young. Hard for Mr. Kilmartin too."

At the mention of Conan's name, Lalage looked away, but

fortunately Madge had moved off to start tidying the room.

" I still don't think she would have tried to hurt her baby. She couldn't have done."

" Well, cook and the others say she did, and they were here, so they should know."

Madge saw the pain in her mistress, her voice softening.

" There, there, love." She came back at once, taking Lalage's hand in her own. " It'll be all right, you'll see. She'll get over it. Commonest thing in the world, you know. Lots of women turn a bit funny after childbirth. Nothing for you to fret yourself about. She's got her husband, and plenty of servants to look after her. Maybe your visit will help too. Nice for her to have one of her own with her for a bit."

" Mr. Kilmartin doesn't expect me to stay longer than a day or two." Lalage withdrew her hand very gently. " He made that quite clear."

" Well, of course. We didn't come for months, did we? Just to have a peep at Miss Prudence, that's all. There, that's the dinner-gong. Off you go, and don't worry. She'll be right as rain before you know it, and you look a fair treat."

Lalage gave a tremulous smile.

" Thank you. Are you going to have dinner in the servants' hall?"

" Yes. Well, supper they call it there. Why?"

" Try to find out more about that night."

" What night?"

" The night Denzil was born." Lalage was torn between impatience, and a desire to conceal the urgent need she had for more details of Prue's behaviour six months before.

" Oh, all right, but I don't know that there's much more they can say."

" Ask, anyway."

Madge pursed her lips as the door closed. She knew her mistress very well, and had seen the change in her although she wasn't sure what had caused it. Miss Lalage always liked to dress well, particular about every detail, but to-night she had seemed extra pernickety. Not for Miss Prue's benefit, that was certain and Conan Kilmartin was a comely man.

She straightened the brushes and comb, suddenly wary and ill-at-ease. There were other things the servants had whispered about, which she hadn't told Miss Lalage. No need to scare her yet with the maids' foolish twittering of what was said to be in the north wing of the house: that part of Amberstone locked away now, and never used. Best forget the whole thing: in two days they'd be back home again.

She glanced at the picture over the bed. A dark-haired, white-skinned woman, in a sea-green gown cut as low as any dress could be. Lips red as rubies, and eyes which followed one round the room. Hard to be a second wife to Kilmartin, once he had loved someone like that.

Madge shook her head.

"And I bet you were a right handful," she said aloud. "A proper tartar, you look, and no mistake. And don't think I believe what was those numskulls below stairs have to say. No chance that you walk about the house at night, m'm, no chance at all. You're dead, and you can't do no harm where you've gone, that's for sure."

*   *   *

Dinner was nearing its end. Crickett, aided by Belinda Isard, Dodo Walsh the first housemaid, and Gussie Worboys, the second housemaid, had served oyster soup, baked fish, mutton cutlets and Soubise sauce, with croûtades of *marrow aux fine herbes* for entrée, and a huge roast sirloin of beef, boiled fowl and celery sauce to follow. After that, there came apples à la Portugaise, Bavarion cream, ices, and tiny biscuits which melted in the mouth.

Lalage normally enjoyed her food, but whilst admiring the excellence of Mrs. Nuttall's fare, found herself merely toying with her meal, whilst Prudence seemed to be eating nothing at all.

Prudence kept her head down, stealing a glance now and then at Lalage. It was some time since she'd seen her cousin, and she had forgotten how lovely she was. She wished with all her heart that she was as ravishing as Lalage. If she were, then Conan might not be so angry with her; less scornful. Yet was that the real reason why he seemed to hate her; because she had grown thin, lifeless, and drab? She wasn't sure: she couldn't remember.

There was the inevitable portrait of Mercedes set above the sideboard. This time she was in riding habit, smiling at the painter as he had caught her image and pinned it down on his canvas. Prue loathed her. She was always there, in every room, critical, sneering, hating the woman who had taken her place. She might just as well have been alive still, for her presence in the house was just as overwhelming.

Conversation was desultory, Prue only answering in a whisper when directly addressed, but as the last of the dessert was served, and only Crickett was left in the room, she said loudly:

"I hope you don't see her too."

Lalage turned quickly, glad to dismiss the knowledge that Conan had been studying her throughout the meal.

"See whom, Prue?"

"Lady Kilmartin, of course." Prue spoke as if she thought Lalage simple. "I often see her. Perhaps if I go to bed now, I'll be asleep before she comes. You'd better do the same."

Crickett opened the door and Prudence slipped away like a wraith. Conan was brusque.

"You may go, Crickett. Tell Tuesday to take some hot milk up to Mrs. Kilmartin's room."

The butler paused for half a second, and Lalage caught a look exchanged between the two men. Not sympathy from a servant to his master, whose wife was sick: something else. But what? Then Lalage and Kilmartin were alone, and he said casually:

"Don't let it concern you. She often says things like that.

We have learned to accept them. I hope you won't be worried
by them."

"I shan't be," returned Lalage with more assurance than
she felt. "I realise Prue isn't herself, and I don't believe in
phantoms."

She took Conan's proferred hand as he led her back to the
sitting-room. The grip was sure and firm, sending a tingling
up her arm. It was a touch she seemed to recognise, evoking a
response with excitement in its depths.

She decided to carry the war into the enemy's camp, for by
now she knew she must stand up to her host.

"If it doesn't distress you, tell me about your first wife. I
heard that she had met with an accident, but no more than
that."

He waited until the coffee had been brought in: tiny por-
celain cups, silver jug, sugar bowl and pot.

"Mercedes? Yes, it was an accident, but it was over two
years ago."

"But it still upsets you to talk of it. I'm sorry, I shouldn't
have asked."

He met her limpid gaze, reading the challenge.

"Very little upsets me, and if it will satisfy your curiosity,
I'll tell you."

The rapier thrust was quick and painful, and Lalage blushed.

"I wasn't being curious."

"No?" He didn't believe her, motioning her to pour. "Black
please, and no sugar. All women are curious. It is a besetting
sin with them, but, since you've travelled so far to see Prudence, I suppose you deserve some reward for your pains."

"Mr. Kilmartin . . . !"

"You called me Conan before."

"Very well, Conan." She was angry, but mostly with herself for letting him get the better of her. "I did not come here
to pry into your affairs, nor do I expect any kind of reward.
You know that perfectly well."

"Do I?" He raised the cup to his lips. "Very well, your

motives were entirely altruistic, but you shall hear about Mercedes nevertheless. It's no secret."

His amusement was gone, his coffee forgotten.

"It happened one afternoon, in the summer. Crickett had brought her a note. Afterwards, when I questioned him, he couldn't remember what the boy was like who gave it to him. He was just a lad, shabbily dressed, but ordinary.

"Crickett took it to my wife, who was in the garden. He said she turned pale, and he thought she was going to faint. It struck him as unusual, for she wasn't a woman given to the vapours. He offered to help her back to the house, but she refused. Then she said she had to meet someone at Devil's Dip."

"Devil's Dip?"

It had a chilling sound, and all at once Lalage was nervous. Somewhere in the deep recesses of her subconscious, another page was being turned. The name was not unknown to her, yet no one had mentioned it until Conan had spoken a second before.

"Yes, it's a hollow: a dell. Just outside the grounds, near to Pope's Wood. There's a pool there, but not much else. The locals avoid it: they say it's haunted." He shrugged. "Nonsense, of course, but the place has had a bad reputation for centuries. In any event, it is isolated, and we don't know to this day why my wife went there, nor whom she was to meet."

"The note?"

"It was never found, and neither was Mercedes."

The quiver was increasing. Lalage could feel her nerve-ends twitch, part of her wishing Conan would stop his story there; another part of her wanting to hear the end of the tale.

"Never found? But, surely, her body . . . ?"

He shook his head.

"No, we didn't find it, not in Devil's Dip, nor anywhere else. A labourer said he saw her going towards it. He was some way off, but he recognised her. When she didn't appear at tea-time, we assumed she was out walking. She often took long walks, so there was nothing to make us suspicious. Later, we realised something was wrong, and the search began."

He was looking up at Mercedes' picture, bitterness forming new lines round his mouth. " The men didn't want to go into the Dip, but they followed me in the end. It was nearly dark by then, for no one supposed she would have stayed there for long, and we had been looking elsewhere."

" And she wasn't there?"

" No, but we found her shoes, hat, and a silk scarf she had been wearing, by the side of the pool, in the reeds."

" You . . . mean . . . she was drowned?" Lalage was stricken with guilt. " Oh, Conan, I'm so sorry, I hadn't realised. You were quite right to upbraid me for asking questions which have caused you pain, and brought back such memories."

For once, his smile was genuine.

" Don't worry, I needed no reminder, and you're not the first to ask about her. You won't be the last. As to whether she drowned, I assume she did, for the centre of the pond is very deep; some say bottomless. The servants, and those in the village, have a different version of her end."

Lalage waited quietly, for it was clear that he hadn't finished.

" They are simpletons, the whole lot of them, and very superstitious, but they believe that there is something under the surface of the pool. They're sure it came out and dragged her down. I told them not to be such fools, but they wouldn't listen, and then . . ."

" Yes?"

She was breathless, tense as she looked at his still face.

" It happened again. Not once, but twice."

" Happened again?"

" Yes, two village girls disappeared. In both instances, some of their personal belongings were found by the water's edge, as in the case of my wife. We don't know why they chose to go there, any more than we know why Mercedes went. All we can tell is that they did go, and they never came back."

" Couldn't the water have been dragged? Wasn't some attempt made to find . . . the bodies?"

" Of course, but, as I say, in the centre of the pool there is no hope of such measures meeting with success."

" That is awful. I don't know what to say, and she looked so . . . well . . . full of life."

" Yes, she was." He glanced back at the painting. " That lace-edged handkerchief she is holding was also found. I forgot to mention it. It had her initials embroidered in one corner."

" I see."

Lalage didn't know what to say to him. She wanted to comfort him, but caution held her back. He didn't look the kind of man who needed it.

" I think the rumours of how she died have affected Prudence." He lit another cigar. " She has brooded on them ,and because some feckless scivvy starts romancing about Mercedes being seen in this house, after her death, Prue is convinced she has seen her."

" You mean some of the servants think they have seen her?"

" No, they just talk about it. It's a topic which goes down well in the servants' hall. No, only Prudence imagines she's seen Mercedes. She is convinced that Mercedes is jealous of her; guilty, because she thinks she has taken her place."

" Well, she has, hasn't she?" Lalage's voice was very low. " And you don't feel about Prue as you felt about your first wife, do you?"

He raised his shoulders negligently.

" Prudence has no reason to feel as she does. Mercedes would have wanted me to marry again. She knew how much I wanted a son."

He threw off the subject as if they had never spoken of it, his tone quite different as he stood up.

" You must forgive me, I have things to do. Will you stay here, or would you prefer to go to the library or the music-room? Do you play the piano?"

" Not very well." She tried to fit in with his changed mood. " But I'll try."

He took her to the music-room, and as soon as the door closed behind him, Lalage caught her breath. It was like coming home: entering a place much-loved and very familiar. Without turning her head, she could have listed every musical instrument down to the humblest recorder. She knew where they were kept, and how old they were. She did not have to lift the seat in the window to know that sheets of music were kept there. She even remembered that there was a scratch on the polished floor where clumsy servants had moved a spinet awkwardly.

It was just as if a curtain had been drawn aside for a second or two, so that she could look backwards to what had been.

Then it was gone, as quickly as it had come, and the room was unfamiliar to her again. She was a stranger in a strange place.

Before bewilderment could become fear, she took her seat at the piano. Her fingers were stiff, and her playing worse than usual. She was about to give up and go to the library instead, when she became aware of a presence. It was a very strong feeling, so real that her hands slipped from the keyboard and she turned quickly expecting to see Crickett, or even Conan, but there was no one there.

But still the sensation of not being alone did not go, and she almost ran from the room, laughing shame-facedly as she reached her bedroom and saw Madge's startled face.

" You see," she said, when she had finished relating her experience, " I'm getting as bad as Prue, or perhaps it's Amberstone, as you said."

" More like it." Madge was terse, patting her grey curls. She was rather proud of her hair, but in moments of stress tended to push invisible wisps into the pins, as if to gird herself for battle. " Told you I was right, didn't I? Said we should never have come here."

It was Lalage's turn to be tidied up, and Madge pulled out

the pins and combs, letting her mistress's hair fall down her back: thick, glossy, curling at the ends. " Real weird goings-on here, I can tell you."

" Oh come! " Lalage was braver now, in the well-lit bedroom, with safe sensible Madge to keep her company. " Next you'll be telling me it is the first Mrs. Kilmartin who's responsible."

Her maid didn't laugh.

" Maybe I will, and here's another thing for you to think about. That girl Sabina Tuesday, came up not five minutes before you arrived. Wouldn't trust that one farther than I could throw her, and if I were Miss Prue, I'd get rid of her straight away."

" But you're not Prue." The brush strokes were soothing, and Lalage's eyes were closed in sensuous pleasure. " What did she want?"

" She asked if you'd lost a handkerchief. Lace-edged, it was."

" Handkerchief?"

" I've told you; with lace round the hem."

" What else? What did you say?"

" Well, that it weren't yours, of course. Got the initials ' M.K. ' worked in silk in one corner. ' Use your eyes, girl,' I said to her. ' Why should Miss Lalage Ashmore have a kerchief with ' M.K ' on it?' She just grinned in that impudent way of hers, and said she'd leave it with me anyway."

" You've still got it? Shew me, quickly! Where is it?"

" All right, all right, no need to get so excited. I haven't lost it. Don't know what's the matter with you to-night, and that's a fact. Here it is. Not yours, is it, so why the fuss?"

Lalage didn't answer. The lace was handmade and very costly, the embroidered letters faultlessly worked. It was exactly the same as that held by the dead Mercedes in the portrait which she and Conan had been discussing not an hour before; the handkerchief which, Conan had said, had been found amongst the reeds in Devil's Dip.

" Help me to bed," said Lalage finally. " I'm tired. It's been a long day."

She let Madge slip the nightgown over her head, feeling the cobwebby material like a cool breeze against her flesh.

" Did that girl say anything else?"

" Plenty, right chatterbox, she is." Madge plumped the pillows up and straightened the coverlet, crisp linen smoothed over it. " Rambling on about some sort of building on the edge of the grounds. A folly, I think she called it. Seems it's known as *The Ruined Tower*, and that a woman who lives in a hut in the woods not far off, spends most of her time there, telling fortunes with Tarot cards. Wicked, I call it: downright un-Christian."

" *The Ruined Tower*." Lalage repeated the words half to herself. " Do you know, I once saw a pack of Tarot cards. They were rather splendid, but I didn't understand what the pictures meant. The woman who shewed them to me said they could be interpreted in different ways, depending who wanted a question answered, and how the cards were laid out. One of the trumps was called *The Ruined Tower*.

" Can't see nothing special in that." Madge was hanging the evening gown up, fluffing out the frilled back. " Maybe it had another name until the wise woman started to tell fortunes there."

" Wise woman!"

" Yes, that's what they call Nanny Peak. She's the one who spends her time there. Seems Miss Prudence is always running off to see her, begging her to help. Tuesday says master doesn't like your cousin going, but she won't listen to him. Must see Nanny Peak every day. The whole village is a bit afraid of her, although they go to her for simples and such like, and to have their futures told. Daft lot. Still, it's all a bit funny, I think."

" Yes, it is." Lalage removed her rings, handing them to Madge to put away. " Conan didn't mention the old woman to me."

" Maybe it didn't occur to him."

" No, I suppose not. It is a coincidence though, isn't it? The folly being called after one of her cards."

"Suppose so." Madge locked the leather jewel box and put it away. "Still, like I said before, maybe it wasn't always called that. One thing's sure though: everyone's wary of the woman."

"Nanny Peak?"

"Aye, right down scared of her, I'd say, even that uppish bit, Sabina. Reckon she's a witch, don't you?"

"There are no such things as witches." Lalage's response was mechanical and not convincing. "You know that."

"I know no such thing." Madge snorted and came to the foot of the bed. "When I was a young 'un we lived in a village in Essex. Essex is the witch county, you know. Plenty of wise women there; wise women or witches, call them what you like."

"Rubbish!"

"No it isn't, and you'll find out I'm right before you're very much older. And here's another thing. You asked me to find out more about the night young Master Denzil was born."

"Yes?" Lalage was eager. "Yes, I did. What did you hear?"

"Well, they said again that missus tried to destroy the babe, and that since that night, it's never been seen by anyone, 'cept master and Mrs. Parkington!"

"No one at all? Not even one of the maids? What about food, and laundry and cleaning? Someone must go to the nursery."

"Only as far as the door. Mrs. Parkington takes stuff from there, and they hear her lock the door after she's shut it." Madge looked a trifle whiter. "One more thing, and I tell you it gave me the shudders when I heard it."

"What? For God's sake, what?"

Then Madge looked harder at her mistress, silent for a whole minute. She'd never seen Lalage so upset as she was now, and there really was something different about her. Not easy to tell exactly where the changes lay, but she seemed to have grown up in the space of a few hours. No longer a young girl, full of thoughtless innocent gaiety, but a woman, very desirable and experienced. Only one thing would make her change in so short a time, and that was a man. Madge's mouth turned down at the corners. There was no man in the house, apart from the servants, except Mr. Conan, and what the maids had said about him had shaken her.

" What's the matter with you? Why don't you answer me?" Lalage almost snapped the words out. " What gave you the shudders?"

Slowly, Madge Commins put the fears out of her mind. It must be her imagination, Miss Lalage was just the same; of course she was. It was simply that here, at Amberstone, everything seemed a bit out of true, as if the world had twisted sideways for a bit. All those lurid tales had got to her, despite her scepticism and she was kicking herself.

" Oh, it's nothing. Forget it."

" I'll do no such thing. What did they say? Which maid?"

Madge sighed. She'd get no peace until she'd told her mistress, and she could have bitten her tongue out for ever starting it.

" Sabina, she was the one. She said that after that night, when Master Denzil was born, there's been something in that north part of the house, where no one ever goes."

" What sort of something?"

Lalage was hanging on to every word, and Madge pulled a face, cursing herself anew. She hadn't meant to let it slip, but now the harm was done.

" They don't know, but those what have been nearest, say it sounds almost like an animal: a dog, maybe, that snarls and scrabbles at the door, trying to fight its way out."

" But there isn't a dog in the house. I expect there are some in the stables, but none inside."

Madge saw Lalage's face, and wanted to put her arms round her and kiss the fears away, but Lalage was no longer her baby. She was a grown woman, with an expression in her eyes which hadn't been there until they had got to Amberstone.

" Is it the first time it's happened?" Lalage lay back against the pillows, her voice quite steady. " Or is this what you and Aunt Ann were talking about? A thing, which has been in this house for a long time."

Madge blew her nose vigorously, fiddling with her hair once more, trying to put off the moment when she had to answer, but there was no getting out of it. Miss Lalage wasn't going to stand any nonsense.

" No, it isn't the first time. Seems it's like what went on about fifty years ago, just after a boy had been born. An heir."

" What happened to him; the boy who was born long ago?"

" Don't know." Madge was apologetic, making for the door. " I'll get your hot milk, it's time you were asleep." She turned her head for a second. " No one knows. He was never seen after the midwife delivered him. Some say he died, others say he was taken to the north wing. Whatever the truth of it is, everyone's story's the same on one point. No one ever set eyes on him again."

Three

Lalage was restless that night. For a long time she lay staring into the darkness, thinking about Prudence, and even more about Conan, seeing his face clearly in her mind, as if he were there, in the room with her.

The next morning she breakfasted alone, for Conan was out, and Prue nowhere to be seen.

" I'm going to have a look at that folly," she said to Madge when she got back to the bedroom. " It's a lovely morning: far too good to stay indoors."

"I'll come with you," said Madge promptly, "though why you want to go to that place, I can't think."

"No, I want to go alone." Lalage's smile softened the rebuff. "And as to why I want to see *The Ruined Tower*, well, it sounds intriguing, don't you agree?"

"No, I don't, and you want to stay away from it, and that woman."

"Really, you must allow me to . . ."

Lalage stopped suddenly, her rebuke unfinished. The door of the room was wide open, and she had the same sense of someone nearby that she had had in the music-room the day before.

"What is it?" Madge didn't like the look on her mistress's face. "Miss Lalage, what's wrong?"

"Is there anyone there: outside, I mean?"

Madge Commins frowned, but she could see that this was no time to argue, moving swiftly towards the door, and poking her head into the passage.

"No one." She came back, more concerned than ever. Miss Lalage was as white as a sheet, almost trembling. "Lovey, there's no one, really. Did you see something?"

"No." Lalage pulled herself together quickly, anxious to avoid questions. "No, I thought I heard a sound. My imagination, I suppose. I shan't be long and don't worry about me. The wise woman isn't going to eat me."

She didn't wait for further protests, leaving Madge biting her lip as she went downstairs and out into the garden. She hadn't told the truth, and she guessed Madge knew it. There had been no sound; just a certainty that someone or something had been standing outside the bedroom, listening.

She forced herself to be rational as she crossed the lawn, turning back once to look at Amberstone. She could see the north wing quite clearly from where she was, and even from that distance it seemed to have a shuttered look about it. She told herself again that she was being fanciful. She hadn't found anything remarkable about that part of the house when she had arrived yesterday, and nothing had changed overnight. She was letting the servants' gossip rattle her nerves.

It took her some time to find the folly, and she might never have come across it, had she not encountered the gardener's boy. He was about fourteen, and wiry, with carroty hair and freckles, answering to the name of Donald Henthorne. His smile was cheery enough until she asked him to direct her to *The Ruined Tower*. Then the grin vanished, and he looked away from her.

"Don't reckon you want to go there, Miss," he said, shuffling awkwardly. "Not a nice sort of place, that. Rose garden's better."

When she persisted, he gave in, shrugging helplessly as she made for the tangled path. He'd done his best, but women were always stubborn, or so his father had told him. Real pig-headed this one had been, but a stunning looker. Even at such a tender age, he'd recognised that.

Lalage looked up at the folly in silence. Although she'd been told what to expect, she hadn't realised how formidable it would be in reality. It was so high, so grey, and so solitary, with its crooked crown and yawning doorway. Lonely and un-welcoming, yet, once again, the sight of it awoke a fleeting sense of knowledge.

She braced herself and went inside. After all, it was only made of stone; a jest of a building which one of Conan's fore-bears had erected in memory of his son. The thought of Conan made her hesitate. He wouldn't have wanted her to come here; she was sure of that. He would have stopped her, physically if it had been necessary, had he known what she had had in mind.

In the dimness, she thought about his kiss, as she had thought about it for many hours during the night. So un-expected, yet so well-remembered. She wondered, briefly, whether he would touch her again, and, if so, what she would do.

Then she saw the candle, and knew that she wasn't alone.

She had never been afraid of anything in her life, and she wasn't going to let the shapeless bundle ahead of her unnerve her now.

"Nanny Peak?"

Her voice was steady and clear, her chin up. First impressions were important and the wise woman was not going to think that Conan Kilmartin's guest was frightened of her.

"Yes." The whisper seemed to roll round the blackness above Lalage. "Aye, I'm Nanny Peak. Wait! That's near enough. Stay there."

Lalage stopped. She could see a large flat stone; the outline of a head, and two hands, hovering over a piece of purple silk.

"Very well." She remained outwardly composed, although the gloom and dank smell of decay was unpleasant; the half-seen body more disturbing still. "I've come to talk to you."

"Oh yes, Missie? What about?"

"Mrs. Kilmartin. She's my cousin, and is unwell. She's very troubled and I'm afraid for her. I'm told she often comes to see you, and I thought perhaps you could tell me what was wrong."

The chuckle was soft, the mittened hands beginning to shuffle a pack of cards.

"For half a sovereign, I might."

"It will be worth it."

"Put it down there; just by that pail."

Lalage obeyed, the coin catching a beam from the candle and winking back at her.

"Well, there's your money. Now, what's wrong with Mrs. Kilmartin? Is it simply the result of childbirth, or not?"

The slight laugh was repeated.

"You might say so, but there's more."

"What else?" Lalage was growing impatient. The old woman hadn't moved, but if she did so, Lalage was strong enough to deal with her. There was no need to be alarmed by some crazy creature who sat in a folly telling fortunes. "I've paid you, so now tell me what I want to know. What else is wrong?"

" Hoity-toity." The whisper wasn't amused now. " You'll wait until I'm ready, or you'll hear nothing."

" I haven't got all day."

" Neither have I."

" Then don't waste time."

The battle became a silent one; then Nanny gave in.

" Spirited, aren't you? Just like the first Mrs. Kilmartin. Lady Mercedes, I used to call her, for she was a real thorough-bred, not like that milksop he's got now. Never left here, you know; my lovely one."

Lalage hung on to her self-control with an effort.

" I don't understand. What do you mean? She was drowned, so Mr. Kilmartin told me."

" Oh yes, she went down into Devil's Dip right enough, but she didn't leave, and the new mistress sees and hears her about the house and grounds. No one else does, of course, but no one else's meant to. Just the second wife, who's not wanted."

" You're talking about a ghost? But that's ridiculous." Lalage tried to dismiss the idea, but she was remembering the strength of her own feeling that someone had been near to her in the music-room and outside her bedroom. " I don't be-lieve it."

" Please yourself, but Mrs. Prudence does. She knows the real mistress doesn't like her here, and intends to get rid of her. Fiery, she was; Lady Mercedes. A true beauty, with hot Spanish blood in her veins; she won't put up with this ninny he's married to for much longer. Worshipped Mr. Conan, she did. She won't let another woman keep him. She often used to come and talk to me about him; never held anything back from me, 'cos she trusted me. Told me how they made love. Passionate, is Mr. Conan, although you'd never think so to see him now; but he was. She'd tell me how he held her in his arms, and how they . . ."

" That's enough!" Lalage had to stop the crooning voice

which was making her feel dirty all over. She didn't want to think of Conan making love to his dead wife. "If she trusted you, you shouldn't be betraying her, especially now that she is no longer alive. And I didn't come to discuss Mercedes, but my cousin."

"Her!" The scorn was obvious. "What must he make of that one in bed, after my queen?"

"Be quiet!" Lalage's anger lent her courage. "I'm not interested in Mr. Kilmartin making love to . . ."

"Oh yes you are." The voice was lower, but very sure. "You'd like to bed with him, if you could. I know."

Lalage went cold all over. How the hateful old woman could possibly have known what extraordinary feelings Conan had aroused in her, she had no idea, but she had to bring the conversation to an end.

"Please, let us talk of Prudence. Tell me about her baby. Why doesn't she look after him, and why won't she even see him? I'm told she has never seen him since he was born, and that only his father and an old nurse care for him. Why?"

"Better not ask. It's not a pretty story. Likely as not you'd scream or faint, if I told you."

"I shall do neither." The chill was increasing, seeping through Lalage's light summer gown, but she wouldn't allow herself to budge an inch. "Tell me."

"Be it on your own head, but don't blame me if you have bad dreams to-night. Well, since you must know, the Kilmartin family has a curse on it. Once every fifty years or so, a male child is born who is not as others are. Not just ordinarily deformed, you understand, but so terrible to look upon that it has to be shut away. The tale goes that on one occasion, the baby wasn't allowed to survive, but it didn't help. Another child of that generation died horribly. No, the cursèd infant has to live its natural span. Sometimes it's only a few months; others it's been years. This one is said to be real bad; not like a human at all. Best if it had died, but it didn't, and his father knew better than to smother it, but his mother weren't so wise. She tried to destroy it. Screamed aloud when she saw it, and then tried to choke it. They dragged her away, and took the thing to the north part of the house, where it would be safe. Shut off, you know; no one goes there now. Una Parkington sees to it: she's got a stomach not easily upset. Trouble is, it's growing stronger now; bigger with each week that passes."

Lalage was frozen to the spot, icy trickles running down her spine. Her mind was shrieking to her not to listen; not to believe. But she couldn't move away, nor let the matter rest.

"But surely . . ."

"Mr. Conan won't do a thing about it. As I say, he knows better than to try. Rich, isn't it? He craved an heir that bad, and now he's got one."

Lalage tried again.

"But . . . but it can't be allowed to li . . . I mean . . . surely. . . ?"

Nanny Peak sniggered.

"This one'll live all right. I've seen it here, in the cards. It'll last its full term. Only question is, what will it do during the time it's here? Now I'll tell you about yourself, since you've come to see me. Move closer, but not too close. Yes, that'll do."

Lalage could see the hands more clearly now, the Tarot Cards being laid out in a horseshoe pattern. Vivid colours, strange figures, odd devices. She was half-mesmerised by them, and the crooning voice.

"There's *The Magician* and *The Hanged Man*. Here's *Temperance*, next to *The Devil*. And there's *The Moon* and *The Star*. Good good. Oh, but here's *The Empress*, next to *Death*."

Fingers hovered, cards shifted. Then the old woman collected them together, a hand outstretched motioning Lalage to take them.

"Shuffle them," Nanny Peak muttered quickly. "Don't like

what I see. Shuffle 'em, and turn some upside down. No, no, not like that. Some one way, some the other. Yes, that's better. Now give 'em back. No! No nearer."

Lalage waited numbly as the cards were spread out again, hearing the deep sigh from out of the darkness.

"No, it's just the same: way I read it."

"Read what?"

"The answers to your questions. That's what you came for, isn't it? To ask questions?"

"Yes, I suppose so, but . . ."

"Well, here's the result." A finger stabbed at the pieces of pasteboard. "As I see it, she'll go soon."

"Who?"

"Your cousin, of course." Petulance at Lalage's stupidity, and another poke at the colourful spread. "Mrs. Prudence's time's nearly up."

"I don't believe it."

"Don't matter whether you do or not; it's the truth. And now I'll tell you about yourself, like I promised. Your life's in danger. There's a man; he's a threat to you. He's nearby; not very far off. Get away soon, while you can. Don't stay too long at Amberstone, or it'll become your grave."

*   *   *

Lalage did not know how she got back to the main gardens. Her knees were like jelly, and she was ashamed to find that her hand was unsteady as she tried to retrieve her skirts from jagged bushes along the path.

As she came to the steps, seeing Amberstone dreaming in the late morning sun, she paused. She couldn't go back yet: she had to have time to pull herself together and clear her mind of ugly thoughts.

She tried to dismiss Nanny Peak's tale of the curse: it was too ludicrous to be true. It was as fantastic as the thought of Prudence trying to kill her own baby. But, if the child was not as others were . . . Lalage checked herself angrily. The wise woman's words had bitten deep.

Aunt Ann had talked of strange, uneasy tales connected with the house; Madge had said she'd been told there was a thing at Amberstone which had been there a long time. Lalage found a rustic seat near the rose-garden and sat down before her legs could give way.

What was the thing? Was it what the local people claimed lay beneath the pool in Devil's Dip, where three people had been drowned? Were they talking about Mercedes, who, although dead, still walked through her old home, according to Nanny and Prue. Or could it be whatever had been taken to the disused wing? It had been there a long time, but Mercedes had only been dead for two years, and Denzil was only six months old, and in his nursery on the third floor.

She was clinging to that crumb of comfort, when Nanny's tale of another birth came back to her, and with it, Madge's awful story of something which snarled like a dog, and tore at a door in an effort to escape. Not like a human at all.

She buried her head in her hands, fighting off stark, primitive fear. It couldn't be true, any of it. It was just a malicious old woman, who'd doted on Mercedes, because the latter had told her of her love-making with Conan, and who didn't like Prue, because she thought her not good enough for the master.

Nothing could live under the water, except small fish, newts and other natural creatures. There were no spirits lurking beneath the sluggish surface, nor was there anything untoward shut up in the north wing.

" You all right, Miss?"

Lalage jumped, startled out of her wits.

The girl who was looking down at her with concern was about fifteen years old, clad in a dun-coloured cotton frock with a sacking apron, hands red and rough. She wore a mob-cap, smudged with soot, and her thin little face was grubby, but there was a glint of compassion in her eyes which Lalage hung on to as if it were a life-line.

"Who are you?"

"I'm Queenie Buncombe, the kitchenmaid." The mouth was a pink triangle, splitting into a smile. "Don't suppose you'd 'ave ever seen me, but cook sent me over to Priddy's Farm to get some more eggs. Me and Gladys aren't allowed upstairs. Suppose we're too dirty for Master's guests." She giggled, not in the least resentful. It was the order of things, and she had accepted her life readily. "Saw you sittin' there. Are you ill? Shall I get 'elp, Miss?"

"No, no." Lalage shook her head, pulling herself together at once. It wouldn't do for a servant to see her alarm. "No, I'm quite all right. It was simply that the sun was rather hot. That basket looks too heavy for you, Queenie. You're the one who needs help."

Queenie laughed again.

"Carried 'eavier things than this before: 'spect I will again. Sure you're not ailing?"

"I have never felt better in my life," returned Lalage untruthfully, "but I should have brought a parasol."

The kitchenmaid cocked her head on one side, her expression far too mature for her age. Buncombe had never known what childhood meant. Once infancy was over, she had started work in a rectory in Oxford and then, later, had moved to the comparative comfort of the kitchens and attics at Amberstone. Always plenty of good food, and only expected to work from six in the morning until mid-night. It was almost like heaven after her first job, where the Rector's wife had made it her business to beat the younger maids regularly once a week to make sure they understood the difference between right and wrong.

"Been to the folly, 'ave you?"

Lalage didn't lie. Buncombe was a servant, and an insignificant one at that, yet she looked sharp. Perhaps she had knowledge which might be useful. She wouldn't have missed a single word of the gossip which went on below stairs.

"Yes, as a matter of fact, I have. A peculiar old woman was

there. At least, I suppose it was a woman. She said she was Nanny Peak, but I couldn't see much of her. It was so dark."

Queenie was glum.

"Oh, she be a woman right enough. An old witch, if you asks me. Folk from the village are 'allus goin' to see 'er to 'ave their fortunes told or to get some potion or other. Right daft, I calls 'em."

"You've never been yourself?"

Buncombe was silent for a moment. Then she said:

"No, never. Once or twice I thought about it, but changed me mind. Nice if she said there was more in life than what I got now, but if she said it were goin' to get worse, then I'm better orf not knowin'."

"Yes." Lalage considered the girl. She really did look more intelligent than most menials, and in any event, it was worth a try. "She told me of a curse on the Kilmartin family, and about a boy who had been born a long time ago, who wasn't . . . well . . . wasn't like other babies."

"Aye." Queenie sighed. "But everyone knows that, Miss. Cursed, they are, the Kilmartins. No doubt about it."

"But you don't believe what Nanny Peak says, surely?"

"About the boy bein' different? Well, maybe I do. You see, once, when I first got 'ere, I. . . ."

"What are you doing here, Buncombe? Why aren't you in the kitchen where you belong?"

Lalage and Queenie started. They had been so engrossed in their conversation that they hadn't heard Conan coming. Queenie turned scarlet, but Lalage rose calmly to the occasion.

"She was asking if I were unwell. I found the sun affected me, and sat down for a while. I was a trifle faint, and Queenie was merely concerned to help me."

The slate-grey eyes turned to the shrinking maid.

"Get back to the house. Go on, be off with you."

"Really, Conan," said Lalage when Buncombe had scuttled off, one arm dragged down by her heavy load, "there was no need to be so sharp with the child. She'd done no wrong."

"Leave the management of my servants to me," he replied briefly, "and if you feel ill, allow me to escort you back to the house."

"I'm perfectly all right now." She was reluctant to take his outstretched hand, but she had no choice. "I can manage quite well on my own."

They walked on slowly, Lalage's crossness at Conan's treatment of Queenie dying down as she stole a look at his profile. If Nanny Peak's tale were only partly true, and if Denzil had some deformity, it was no wonder that Conan was bitter and withdrawn. Prue hardly rational; a son not normal. It would turn any man sour. She would like to have offered him sympathy, but he wouldn't have wanted that, and if the wise woman had told her a pack of lies, she would only make herself appear ridiculous.

Nevertheless, when she spoke again, her voice was gentler.

"Your home is a lovely place. How proud you must be of it."

"Yes."

No enthusiasm or pride; just a monosyllabic confirmation of his feelings.

"There must be many tales connected with it. It is so old."

He turned his head, eyes almost blind as they looked into hers.

"Only stories made up by the ignorant. Lalage, we have guests for dinner to-night." The subject was changed abruptly. "Dr. Leeford, with Colonel Philpot and his wife, Cressida. Sir James Laurie and Lady Lucinda will be there too, with a visitor they have staying with them. A French nobleman of some sort, I believe. I can't remember his name."

"I shall look forward to meeting them."

"I wish to God they weren't coming, but it's difficult to live in complete isolation in a place like this." The tone changed again. "Do what you can to make Prudence look respectable, will you? It is shameful when she comes down looking like a washerwoman."

" Yes, of course I will."

They were in the hall by that time. Conan's inner anger seemed to leave him quite suddenly. She thought his hand was touching hers, but she couldn't be sure. All she knew was that she wanted him to kiss her again; to hold her against him. The formality they had shewn one another was all wrong; there should have been intimacy and love.

The moment faded away, as other moments had done. She was Lalage Ashmore again, and she had only just met Prue's husband. Yet she didn't move away at once, and neither did he.

They just stood for a while looking at each other. Finally, Lalage whispered an excuse and made her way upstairs, knowing that Conan was watching her go.

When she reached her bedroom, Madge was there, ready to help her prepare for luncheon, and full of her latest tit-bits of gossip.

The thick curls were tidied; busy fingers, busier tongue.

" You know what's said about that part of the house where no one goes?"

" Mm."

Lalage was selecting a perfume, her mind still full of the long minute with Conan.

" Well, Gussie Worboys was up here cleaning this morning, and we got to talking. You'll never guess what she said."

Lalage forced Kilmartin out of her mind, trying to pay attention.

" No, what did she say?"

" Well, it seems that one or two of the servants dared Worboys to go up to the door which shuts off the north wing. Bit spiteful, really, 'cos she's as afraid as a kitten anyway. Still, they bullied her into it, and off she went. Eleven o'clock at night, it was, and no one about."

" Poor Worboys. How unkind people can be."

Madge ignored the sympathy for the luckless Gussie.

" Well, she got there, although she said she was shaking like a leaf. Just about to go back to the kitchen when she heard sounds."

The perfume bottle was replaced: Lalage extremely calm, almost disinterested.

" Yes?"

Madge was not put off. She knew her mistress very well. Miss Lalage might pretend indifference, but she was dying to hear the rest.

" Aye, an awful noise too, according to Gussie. Like an animal, behind that door. Clawing at the wood too, as if it was fighting to get out. Gussie screamed and flew back to the kitchen. Took 'em half and hour before they could get the lass to stop crying."

For a moment nothing was said. Lalage was watching a bird, perched on the window sill, seeing the blue sky, broken by fleecy white clouds. There was the hum of bees, a faint breeze moving the curtains and sending up a hint of fragrance from the roses which grew on that side of the house. All so normal and ordinary and beautiful.

Then she looked at Madge.

" Just her imagination, I should think."

" Funny sort of imagination. I reckon we ought to get away from here, and the sooner the better."

" Well, we shan't be here long, and we shall be all right. Don't worry: nothing can hurt us. We'll be safe enough."

She left a deflated Madge, pausing at the top of the stairs. Safe? She would have laughed, if she had had any humour left in her. Devil's Dip; the dead Mercedes; the north wing; Conan.

Nobody was safe at Amberstone.

*   *   *

Lalage and Madge could find nothing in Prudence's wardrobe which would fit her.

" I reckon your red silk, don't you, Miss Lalage," said Madge finally. " Give her a bit of colour, and she's about your size now."

Prue was apathetic as the two women got her into the Paris gown, listless and uncaring as they tinted her cheeks, dressed her hair with combs and artificial flowers, and touched her wrists with perfume.

" That's better." Madge was beaming with self-complacency. "Looks a real picture now, doesn't she?"

Lalage considered her cousin thoughtfully. The costly dress had a swathe of lace round the low neckline, and frill after frill floated down from the small bustle. The powder and rouge had give Prudence a false glow, but her fingers were busy tearing at the delicate fan clutched in her hands. She might look a picture, but inside, Prudence Kilmartin was on the brink of collapse.

" What is it, sweet?" asked Lalage finally. " Something is worrying you terribly. Can't you tell me what it is?"

She exchanged a quick look with Madge, whose smile had died. She too had seen by now that her handiwork was really wasted.

" Won't you let me help?"

" You can't." Prudence's voice was flat. " Nobody can. I saw her again this afternoon, by *The Ruined Tower*."

" Saw who?"

" Mercedes." One of the spines of the fan snapped as Prue's fingers tightened. " She wants me to go. She won't let me stay here much longer."

The others looked at one another helplessly, but then the dinner-gong went, and there was no more time for questions.

Desmond Leeford turned out to be an elderly man with bushy side-whiskers and a full beard. He took Lalage's hand and said gruffly:

" Well, you won't be a patient of mine, will you, nor my friend Morefield's either, come to that? Healthy young filly, by the look of you."

Lalage was taken aback by the blunt greeting, but Leeford gave a rumbling laugh.

"Don't take any notice of me, child, I'm too old for gallantry. Still, I'm not so far gone that I don't recognise a beauty when I see one." The twinkling black eyes lost their smile. "Only here for a short time, eh? Just as well. Better get back to London as soon as you can."

He walked off, but before Lalage could follow him to demand an explanation for his warning, Conan was introducing her to Colonel Philpot, jolly and rubicund, and his short, sparrow-like wife, dressed in strident green, with too many necklaces round her scrawny neck.

"You've done well with Prudence." Kilmartin waited until they had a brief moment alone. "She looks almost human. Let's pray to God that she keeps her mouth shut, and then we'll be all right."

"Conan, I really think . . ."

"And you. . . ." His mouth moved slightly. "You look very charming, and it's no wonder that old Philpot's eyes are bulging out of his head."

She seized upon his good-humour, knowing she might not get a second chance.

"You said I had to go in two or three days."

"Did I?"

"You know you did. Do you think I could remain a while longer? I really am concerned about Prue, and perhaps I could help her if I stayed. You said I'd done well to-night, didn't you?"

He gave a slight laugh, acknowledging her wiles.

"I doubt if you can really help, but stay if you wish." The grey eyes moved slowly over her. "Even if you cannot be useful, you are beyond doubt ornamental."

He raised her hand to his lips, fingers tightening over hers. She felt as if they were alone in the room, despite the hum of conversation, fighting to keep her face expressionless lest one of the more perceptive guests should notice that she was holding his hand as tightly as he held hers.

Then Sir James and Lady Lucinda arrived, and Conan was the perfect host again. James Laurie was middle-aged and kindly looking, holding an important Government post; his wife a strapping woman, bearing a remarkable resemblance to the horses which she rode and bred.

"And you must meet the Comte de Lys," said Conan, indicating the tall, elegant man behind Lucinda. "Sir, this is Miss Ashton, my wife's cousin."

"*Dieu*, Lally! And what on earth brings you here?"

"Gaston!"

Lalage felt a sudden rush of relief, as if the whole fearful world of Amberstone had been washed away in the aggressive normality of Gaston Delorme's presence. Spectres could never survive with Gaston about; he was far too sensible, at least, as far as they were concerned.

She had known him since childhood. Their families, living in Paris, had been old friends. They'd played together, quarrelled together, and grown up together, and she gave a small sigh as she took in every inch of him.

Gaston had very blond hair, with a skin gently tanned, making his yellowish eyes brighter than jewels. His nose and mouth were without fault, his jaw firm. Far too handsome for his own good, Aunt Ann had said, and she had been right. Lalage and he hadn't seen each other for some time, and she seemed to be seeing him with new eyes.

The tales which were told of the rich comte did not bear dwelling upon, but at least his dubious pursuits were earthy and straightforward.

"You know one another?"

Lalage could sense Kilmartin's displeasure when Gaston kissed her.

"Oh yes, for a very long time." The comte's accent was barely perceptible. He had spent three years at Oxford, idling his time away, according to Ann, but she admitted it had improved his English, if not his morals. "Lalage and I were

C

brought up together. She was a horrible child, as I recall. All bones and teeth, with an impossible temper."

" Gaston! "

" Calm, *ma petite*, calm. Time has done wonders for you, don't you agree Mr. Kilmartin?"

" Indeed."

Conan's voice was without emotion, but he soon detached the comte and led him off to meet Dr. Leeford, whilst Lalage struggled through small talk with Lucinda.

But after dinner, and when the men were done with their port and cigars, Gaston contrived to get Lalage into a corner where coffee was served to them, and where she could watch uneasily Prue's rising tension. Prue had hardly spoken during the meal, and it was obvious that the company was a strain on her. Lalage had had the dreadful feeling that her cousin was about to burst into hysterical cries.

" Well, my love, that is done." Gaston's smile was a caress. " What an absurd ritual it is. I would much rather have been talking to you. Now tell me, why are you at Amberstone?"

" Prue's my cousin. I'd heard that she wasn't well, and so I came to see her."

The comte turned his head.

" Ah yes, the frightened Mrs. Kilmartin. I'd forgotten you were related."

" Frightened?" She picked him up at once. " Why do you say that?"

" Because it is obvious, isn't it?"

It was no good pretending with Gaston.

" Yes, I suppose so, and what about you? Why are you here, of all places?"

The lazy topaz eyes turned back to her.

" You might well ask. *Maman* had prepared so tiring an itinerary for me, a fruitless effort to reform me, you understand, that I decided to escape to England for a while. I expect she is very angry with me, because I didn't tell her I was going."

"You are impossible; you always were."

"Yes, but the good God has punished me, because for some reason, which entirely escapes me, I find myself staying with a woman who not only looks like a mare, but makes very similar noises when she laughs."

"It serves you right." Lalage was still weak with relief to find him there. Nothing would go wrong with Gaston about; he would see to that. "But surely there is some attractive daughter or maidservant with whom you could dally to alleviate the boredom."

"Alas, no daughters, and I never molest servants, as you know. Tell me, why have the English never learned to make coffee? This is quite appalling. It tastes like liquid mud."

"Yes, it does rather. I should leave it if I were you. I suppose you haven't mended your ways since we last met. Do you still gamble as much?"

"More, but always with success."

"And do you flirt still?"

"Consistently. And you, my little Puritan?"

"No, I do not!"

"Liar." He gave a soft laugh. "I noticed that our host did not like it when I greeted you. Why was that I wonder?"

"I'm sure you're mistaken." Her colour was a little higher and she avoided his eye. "But perhaps he didn't think your salutation was quite suitable for the drawing-room. You always kiss a woman as though you are about to make love to her."

"I usually am, but I don't think it was disapproval. Much more likely that he was envious, and why not? In that gown, any man would want to seduce you."

"Gaston! You mustn't say things like that, especially in England, and in such company. People simply wouldn't understand."

"I expect they would. I find people much the same the world over. However, I'll try to curb my tongue, and my desire, if it will please you. Let us talk of other things."

"Yes, let's."

Lalage relaxed, but her relief was short-lived.

"Why is your cousin losing her wits?"

"She's not!"

He put his cup down and said reflectively:

"I think I preferred you when you were ten years old. You were so devastatingly honest in those days."

"Oh very well!" Lalage was put out, yet in a way she wanted to talk to somebody about Prue, and Gaston had always been very practical. "If you must know, she isn't as she was. It's the result of childbirth . . . I think."

"I see." He was reflective. "And when are we to see the much-wanted heir? My hostess has told me of the sad loss Mr. Kilmartin sustained, and how he married Prudence to get a son. Poor girl. Shall we see the child to-night?"

Delorme watched Lalage's colour seep slowly away. Her skin was like priceless alabaster, and just as pale. His eyes narrowed.

"*Chérie?* What is it?"

"Nothing. For goodness sake stop asking questions."

"You're not a very good liar after all." He took her hand in his. "Now, for my part, I have made a study of deception, and brought it to a fine art."

"I'm sure you have," she retorted tartly. "Do be quiet, Gaston, I want to think."

"Mm." He still held her hand, long slender fingers strong against hers. "When you have stopped thinking, and want to talk truthfully, you know where I am."

Lalage didn't reply. She was once again aware of Conan's forbidding face. He didn't like her closeness to the Frenchman; liked even less the affectionate gestures. She didn't know whether to be glad that he was interested, or sorry that he had noticed them.

"Gaston, I must go and talk to the others. They will think it rude if I spend the whole evening with you."

"The others won't care, but our host will. He doesn't approve."

He saw the flicker of shock in her, and his hold tightened again.

"So cold," he murmured. "Poor Lalage, don't fall in love with Kilmartin, for I am assured by Lucinda that he is a terrible man."

"Don't be absurd." She pulled her hand away angrily. "I'm not in the least in love with him. What an outlandish notion."

"Is it?" He was quizzical. "I'm not blind, and you do not know how to conceal your thoughts. Oh, by the way, have you seen the ghost yet?"

He saw her pupils widen; saw the gripping of the arm of the chair until her knuckles were like stone.

"How did you hear about that?"

"From the same source as all my knowledge of Amberstone and those who live here. Lady Lucinda has told me about Mercedes, and her habit of wandering round the house at night. Indeed, she has told me so much about her, that I feel I know her well."

Lalage raised her head to Mercedes' portrait.

"She's dead. You can't possibly know her."

"Dead? Is she? Some say she wants to kill her successor, and judging by what I see in that painting, I would say that she was more than capable of doing so."

"How I wish these mischief-making servants would keep their ridiculous ideas to themselves," said Lalage hotly. "That's where Lady Lucinda gets her information from; below stairs gossip, and you know how unreliable that is. She is stupid to listen to it."

"Oh, I don't know." His mouth moved in a faint smile, but he was watching her anger carefully. "It's such a temptation to listen, isn't it? Here we have an old house about which odd stories are told: a harsh but good-looking master, and a girl-bride who is apparently terrified of something. A ghost? Or is it because her husband beats her? All the makings of a romance. You'd better be careful."

" Of what?" She was sharp, irritation mounting. " Why should I be careful?"

He leaned forward and kissed her, ignoring the fact that Conan Kilmartin was coming towards them.

" Of Mercedes, of course. Make sure you don't get in her way, or she may not stop at killing your cousin. She may consider you a nuisance too."

Four

Lalage sat up in bed, hugging her knees. She was thinking about Gaston and his unexpected appearance at Amberstone, but there was more to it than surprise. She had known him for so long, that she had always taken him for granted. He was like a brother, to be teased or cajoled, depending on her mood.

She had accepted that he was handsome, because everyone had said so, but it wasn't until that night that she herself had really realised just how good looking he was. He hadn't seemed at all like a brother, particularly when he had kissed her.

It was another small disturbance in her life; another stable prop cracking under her.

Conan hadn't regarded Delorme as her brother either. Her thoughts moved on to Conan. He had been angry, and jealous too, as the watchful Gaston had seen. She had had no experience of real emotions before, but she'd recognised that. It was quite a different thing from the mannered protestations of the young men with whom she had carried on harmless flirtations in the past. They had known the rules of the game, and so had she. Deep feelings played no part in those diversions, yet when Lalage had seen Kilmartin's face, she had been in no doubt of what he was thinking.

It must be the effect of Amberstone. She had been warned about the place, but had ignored the dangers. Her tranquil, well-ordered life was being turned upside down, first by Conan, and now by Gaston. It was most uncomfortable, and she didn't like it.

She lay down, pulling the pillow under her head, resolutely courting sleep. She was behaving like a silly school girl, and the sooner she came to her senses the better. It would be different in the morning; she would make sure of that. Conan would simply be Prue's husband, and she would keep him strictly at arm's length, and Gaston would simply be . . . well . . . Gaston, and not a disturbingly attractive man who'd made her pulse quicken alarmingly.

But sleep wouldn't come, and in an effort to break her train of thought, she got out of bed and went to the window, only to find a fresh puzzle awaiting her.

Looking down, she could see a man astride a horse, the moon giving enough light for her to identify him. Then he was gone, galloping off into the darkness. She stood there for quite a while, thinking. Why on earth was Conan out so late? Where could he possibly be going at two o'clock in the morning?

It was then that the idea came to her. With Conan out of the house, there was only one person guarding Denzil, and there was a fair chance that Mrs. Parkington would be asleep. It was worth investigation at any rate, and she took her candle and went up to the third floor.

No one had told her exactly where the nursery was, yet instinctively she knew how to find it, hesitating for a second, the familiar unease returning. How had she known where to look?

She pushed that question aside; there was no time for it

now. She half-expected to find the door of the nursery locked, as the servants said it always was, but to her surprise it was open.

She waited again, to see if there were any sounds, but everything was quiet. Then she turned the handle very gingerly and a second later was inside the room. It was like any other nursery, with a high fire-guard, a nursing chair by the hearth, two painted tallboys, a truckle bed, and long blue curtains at the windows.

There was no one there. Mrs. Parkington must have gone up to her own room, or perhaps to the kitchen to get tea. The narrow bed hadn't been slept in; it was neat and tidy and impersonal, as if it didn't belong to anyone.

Lalage wasted no more time. Mrs. Parkington might return at any minute, and she moved quickly to the cot, draped in muslin, shielding its small occupant.

She bent over, gently pulling back the cover, holding the candle lower to see Prue's baby.

She felt a stab of pure terror well up inside herself, the candle shaking and dropping spots of wax on her cold hand.

It wasn't Denzil in the crib, but a life-sized china doll, holding up stiff little arms, as if begging her to pick him up. In the wavering light, the toy looked horrible: blue glass eyes shining eerily under lashes made of silk; pouting rosebud lips; chubby cheeks; even a dimple in the chin.

She smothered a cry and ran, slamming the nursery door behind her, not caring if anyone heard or not. In the safety of her own room, she sat shaking on the side of the bed, one thought hammering in her brain.

If there was a doll in Denzil's cot, where on earth was Denzil himself?

*   *   *

At four-thirty, Prudence heard the door of her bedroom open. She had not slept, in spite of her fatigue, and there were tears still wet on her cheeks.

The evening had been a disaster for her, with Conan's condemning look following her round the room, his guests trying not to see what a hopeless mess she was. Even kind Lalage's efforts to make her pretty had been no use.

She had watched her cousin with the good-looking man who was Sir James's guest. They had held hands for a while, she had noticed, and he had kissed her, even though the room had been full of people. She had also been aware that Conan had seen them, his anger obvious as he had turned away to speak to someone else.

"Now, she sat up quickly, holding the bedclothes round herself for protection.

"Who . . . who is it?"

"It is I, my dear. Who were you expecting?"

"Conan!" The fear didn't go. Rather, it increased as he crossed the room and put his candle down. "What is it? What's wrong?"

"Nothing that I know of." The flame of the candle made the part of his face which she could see look harder than ever, as if he were one of the statues from the garden, come to seek her company. "Should there be?"

"No, but why are you here? What do you want?"

"What do husbands usually want when they visit their wives?" He sat on the side of the bed, regarding her meditatively. "I'm sure that even you will not find that question hard to answer."

He saw her shrink away from him, but he didn't move. She did not look well: not like Lalage, with her glowing good health, and bright beautiful eyes. Lalage, whose mouth was perfection, and whose body would have roused envy in Aphrodite herself. Yet, in the half-light, Prudence's fair hair was a cloud about her shoulders, and the smudges beneath her eyes not so apparent.

"No, Conan, no! I can't!"

"Why not? Do you find me so repulsive?"

She wanted to say yes, and to push him away, but she could

do neither. Words would not come, and her hands were paralysed. In any event, what was the use? He was her husband, and he had the right to make demands. That was what he had paid her father for, and there was nothing she could do about it now.

She did not resist as he undid the ties of her nightgown and pulled it over her head. Naked, she felt totally vulnerable, dreading what was to come. When his hand touched her, she whimpered.

"For Christ's sake!" He was filled with subdued fury. "What's wrong with you now?"

"It's too soon." She tried again to put him off. "You know it is. Much too soon."

"After the child's birth? Don't be ridiculous, that was six months ago. Do you expect me to live like a monk?"

"No, but . . ."

"You are my wife." He ground the words into her mind like fragments of glass. "Mine, to take when I want to."

"I'm not well." She tried to edge away, moving slightly so that his hand could not touch her skin. "I'm ill; everyone says so."

"You are well enough to make love," he returned curtly. "We are not going to scale a mountain."

"But . . . I . . . can't . . ."

"It doesn't have to be like this."

The profile was still visible by the candle-light. It had in no way softened, and his voice was rougher than ever.

"We could love like others do."

"No!"

The candle was snuffed out, and she felt his hands on her shoulders, bruising and punishing as he dragged her nearer. When she finally found enough strength to fight him, he hit her hard across the face, pinning her to the mattress.

"Very well." His voice was icy in her ear. "If you want another battle, so be it."

Prudence did not appear at breakfast the next morning, and Lalage could not take her eyes off the red marks down one side of Conan's face.

He caught her staring at him, and said coldly:

" Yes, they are scratches. No doubt you wonder why."

She felt a tightening inside herself. His anger was raw, but she sensed it wasn't for her, yet she didn't want him to go on.

" I'm sorry," she said stiffly, " I hadn't meant to . . ."

" Oh, but I'm sure you're curious." He was buttering toast, lips a thin line. " As I said before, all women are curious. Well, this is your precious cousin's doing. I was not welcome when I went to her last night."

Lalage felt as though someone had struck a blow at her heart. It was ludicrous of her to imagine that Conan did not have normal relations with Prue; they had a six-month old son to prove it. She cursed herself for imagining that because Conan had kissed her, and was angry because of Delorme's attentions to her, he had ceased to sleep with his wife. She felt sick, and wished she could get away from his bitterness and her own pain, but the meal had only just started.

Finally she said:

" I don't think you should . . ."

" Betray the secrets of the marriage bed?" He was caustic. " There are no such secrets. Everyone here knows what my wife thinks of me."

She sat mute, trying to blot out of her mind the picture of Conan and Prue together: then Conan said quietly:

" I'm sorry, I shouldn't vent my feelings on you."

" It doesn't matter."

" But it does. It is ill-mannered, if nothing else."

" I don't mind. I understand."

He got up and helped himself to eggs and bacon, turning to look at her pensively.

" Do you? I wonder."

" She isn't herself."

" Even when she was, she was scarcely warm-blooded." He took a sip of black coffee. " Not as you are."

She hadn't forgotten her promise to herself not to let him draw her into that web again. It was too dangerous: besides, Conan was still very much Prue's husband.

" You can't be sure." Her smile was an effort; keeping her tone light more difficult still. " I might be very cold-blooded, for all you know."

" You didn't appear so when you were talking to Delorme last night."

In spite of herself, his sharp comment warmed her.

" I've known him a long time."

" And regard him as a brother? Is that what you are saying?"

" Not exactly. Really, this is a most unsuitable conversation to be having first thing in the morning. Besides, we hardly know one another."

He smiled gently and with knowledge.

" A fact which could be remedied, if it were true."

She wasn't sure how to answer that, only aware that it aroused in her some queer certainty that he wasn't making idle talk. To turn away from the issue, which she knew she mustn't pursue, she said in a small voice:

" I thought I wasn't welcome here."

" I told you yesterday that you could stay if you wished."

She was about to reply, when she saw the sombre figure of Una Parkington pass by the window of the breakfast-room, and suddenly the fright of the night before had her in its grip once more. She was back in the dark nursery, candle-light gleaming on the brass rail of the guard; the low, cretonne-covered chair; the cot, and the object which had lain in it.

She knew she was ashen, praying that Conan wouldn't notice, but he did.

" You're trembling. Why?"

"It's nothing. I have a headache. If you'll forgive me, I'll go for a walk. That will clear it."

He rose, moving towards her until they were no more than a few inches apart. The thought of the cot slipped out of her mind: all she could think about was his nearness. Just briefly, she wished Gaston were there, for he would never let the situation get out of hand. Then Gaston vanished too.

"Yes, of course, Liane."

"Liane?"

That woke a chord too, but she didn't know why.

"Did I say Liane? I meant Lalage. I'm growing absent-minded."

She knew he wasn't. Conan Kilmartin was very much the master of his own thoughts, but it didn't seem to matter now. She was on the point of raising her face so that he could kiss her, when he said:

"I will see you at luncheon, and Lalage."

She was brought back to earth with a bump, thanking God she hadn't had time to make a spectacle of herself.

"Yes?"

"I advise against going to the folly. It might be unsafe."

She grasped at the new subject with gratitude.

"I wasn't going there, but the old woman seems harmless enough."

"You've seen her then?" He was watching her closely. "I hadn't realised that. And what did you make of her?"

"She was what I had expected. Pretends to tell fortunes and loves to frighten the villagers."

She wasn't going to let him know Nanny Peak had frightened her too.

"I see. Well, nevertheless, I should keep away from her if I were you. I don't believe that she has 'the power', as they say, but sometimes her predictions come true."

"Oh?"

"Yes. I met her once, near *The Ruined Tower*. I told her to get off my land, or it would be the worse for her. She just laughed at me, and said she'd pay me out for trying to get rid of her. She said she'd take from me the thing I cared for most."

He paused, frowning, not seeing Lalage.

"I thought she meant Amberstone, but I was wrong. Two days later, Mercedes disappeared. The woman was right: I had lost what I cared for most—a mother for my son. Keep away from her, or who knows what may happen to you?"

*   *   *

At seven o'clock that evening, Fanny Thurston announced that she was going for a walk. She looked round at her family with affection. Ma, who had provided a good hot dinner from her blackened cooking pot, making the most of the bit of bacon left over from the last pig-killing; home-grown cabbage, and a spotted pudding. Only one utensil over the fire, so each item had to be wrapped carefully in its own piece of bleached cloth, and lowered at exactly the right time into the boiling water. But for all that it had been tasty, if somewhat sparse, only Pa getting anything like a decent portion.

Fanny didn't begrudge him the lion's share; it was his due. Worked hard from dawn till dusk in the fields, always giving his wages over to Ma on a Friday night. He looked up as she spoke, smiling kindly as he drew a luxurious mouthful of cheap tobacco from his clay pipe.

"Don't be long, lass," he warned. "Just a wee while, no more."

"Oh, pa! I'm goin' on sixteen now."

"You're still fifteen, and my girl. Now mind what I say, and keep away from the Dip."

Fanny's responding smile faded. She was very pretty, with a lot of soft brown hair and wide velvety eyes. True, her cotton frock was old and patched, but the apron was scrubbed as white as snow, and she'd managed to save a penny to buy a piece of scarlet ribbon from the travelling salesman who came to Foxgrove once a month. She'd felt a bit guilty, wasting precious money on frivolities when her mother had had to scrape the last ha'penny from her pocket to buy much-needed cups and plates. Still, it did look real nice, holding her curls back, and she had felt a warm sense of well-being until her father had mentioned Devil's Dip.

In common with all those who lived hugger-mugger round the village green, some in brick built cottages with thatched roofs, some in stone boxes with blue-slated top-knots, Fanny was in dire fear of the Dip.

" Oh, I will, pa, I will."

She was earnest, anxious to get away, for her mission was an important one, and she didn't want her parents to have second thoughts about letting her go. She edged to the door, praying her mother wouldn't tell her to mend her torn night-gown, or to go and look after the younger children playing outside by the pig-sty.

Tom Thurston nodded, and went back to his paper. Fanny was a good girl; she could be trusted. Emily Thurston, darning a large hole in one of her son's socks, inclined her head too. Couldn't blame her daughter for wanting to get out of the poky cottage, with its single living-room and two bedrooms, which had to accomodate two adults and six children of assorted ages and sex. It might have a rag rug on the floor, and pots of geraniums in the window, and be a good deal better than some of her neighbour's hovels, but it was still dirt poor.

She hadn't forgotten what it felt like to be young, and although Fanny believed her mother ignorant of her interest in Roger Wheddon, one of the farm lads, Emily hadn't missed any of the signs. Flushed cheeks, tidier appearance, fussing over her hand-me-downs as if life itself depended on them being just right. Oh yes, Fanny was experiencing love for the first time, and her mother sighed.

Pity that that heart-stopping feeling couldn't go on forever, but it never did. Once the flutter of courtship was done, it was marriage, with a few sticks of furniture, rent taking most of the income, children coming year by year, and the constant worry of trying to make the flat purse stretch far enough to provide enough food for ever-hungry mouths.

Unaware of the disadvantages of the future, Fanny sang to herself as she left the green and went up the dusty path towards Pope's Wood. She was blithely happy on that hot August evening, thinking of her Roger, wondering if he were thinking of her too. She wouldn't be able to see him that night, because she had another job to do, but he'd be there tomorrow, same as usual, waiting by the big oak just inside the woods.

Nanny wasn't in her own cottage, but Fanny was not put out. Everyone knew that when she wasn't at home, Nanny was in the folly on Mr. Conan's land, and so she turned and made for the grounds of Amberstone, still contented.

She believed implicitly in what Nanny Peak had to say, for hadn't the old woman told her, only a year ago, that within weeks she would meet someone who'd steal her heart, and, sure enough, not a month later she'd met Roger.

She'd told Mrs. Poke that her husband wasn't long for this world too, and, lo and behold, within a few days, Abraham Poke was lowered into his grave, dead of a fever.

Fanny stopped outside *The Ruined Tower*. It really was rather grim, and she was scared that the top of it might fall on her if she didn't hurry up and get inside, so taking a deep breath she scuttled through the door, blinking in the pitch blackness.

It took a second or two before she could see well enough to make her way warily to the centre of the folly. There was no candle alight, so it seemed Nanny had not arrived, but Fanny had to wait, for her question this time was important. She wanted to know how long it would be before her wedding day. The old woman would know; she knew everything. Fanny had no money to pay her, but Nanny knew that when the next pig was killed, she'd get her tribute from the Thurston family.

At first, Fanny wasn't particularly afraid. The folly was

rather frightening because it was so quiet and dark, but she'd been there plenty of times before, and the wise woman wouldn't be long. It wasn't until she heard the slight noise that her heart jumped into her mouth.

There was a light now, burning warmly, bringing the grey stones into focus, but it wasn't the walls of the tower which made Fanny blanch and caused her to back away, one hand rammed across her mouth.

She moaned, rooted to the spot for what seemed an eternity, as she waited for what was coming towards her. Then, with a supreme effort, she forced her legs to work, and ran screaming from the folly.

It was Donald Henthorne who found Fanny the next morning. The villagers had been searching for the girl since she had failed to return home, but until that moment their efforts had been fruitless.

He raced back to Amberstone, hardly coherent as he blurted out the dreaded news. The other servants followed him back across the gardens to the tower, chattering, and demanding to know whether he had lost his senses, but when they reached the beech tree, they could see for themselves that he had been right.

From one of the lower branches, Fanny Thurston's body dangled a few feet from the ground, her face too dreadful to look at, a thin cord round her young neck and looped over the wooden arm of the tree.

"Well, everyone knows why she did it," said Sabina Tuesday some hours later. "Nanny must have told her Roger Wheddon wouldn't marry 'er, and since she'd lain with 'im, the disgrace were too much for 'er."

Madge and Lalage regarded the girl with acute dislike. It was clear that the death of another human being meant no more to her than an exciting topic of conversation.

"Do you know that for sure?" asked Lalage finally, wishing the girl would go away. "If you've no proof, you shouldn't say such things, especially now that Fanny is dead."

The narrow face crinkled up.

"No proof, of course." The tone was as gloating as the eyes. "But everyone knew 'ow she felt about Roger. Used to go walkin' of an evenin'. Don't suppose they spent all their time just talkin', do you?"

She slipped off, and Madge said tightly:

"Never knew a wench I turned against so much as I do that one. Real nasty piece, she is. But she's not the only one who says Fanny Thurston was not all she should be. Whole staff's agog, and that's a fact. It's her poor mother I feel sorry for. Got another five at home, I'm told, but Fanny were her first-born. She'll not forget that."

Later, in the morning-room, Lalage encountered Conan, just returned from a ride. She could feel her throat closing, his very presence awakening in her that oddness, as if she were moving out of the real world into another, where almost anything could happen.

"You look pale," he said abruptly. "What's wrong?"

"Nothing." She wasn't even aware of his sharpness; only that he was very near to her. "Tuesday has been telling Madge and me about that girl who hanged herself."

"Fanny Thurston. Little fool!" He flung his gloves and whip aside. "She'd no business to be near the folly. I suppose she went to that damned old harridan to have her future told."

"The servants say she was in love with a farm boy."

"Love!" His laugh was curt. "She was fifteen. What could she possibly know about love?"

"Do you have to be old to understand love?"

His temper was gone, and he was looking at her properly for the first time since he had entered the room, his mouth softening.

"No, I suppose not. You know all about love, don't you, and you are young."

"Not fifteen."

"No, but not much more."

" Twenty-one is a lot more."

He smiled, the corners of his eye creasing in amusement.

" So it is."

She felt his hand against her face, her mouth dry as ashes.

" Beautiful Liane." His voice was barely audible. " How marvellous you are to look at. Do you know how much I would like to take you to bed?"

Her lips parted. She wanted to protest, but she couldn't speak. Couldn't even ask why he did not call her by her right name.

" You'd like that too, but the conventions we have to live by now would hold you back, wouldn't they?" He put his head on one side. " But you can forget nice customs, here at Amberstone. It is not like any other place on earth; it knows how to keep its secrets. Surely you remember that. We could lie together again, you and I, and no one would ever know."

Lalage was helpless. His voice, his touch, were holding her in thrall, and she couldn't break away. Even her mind was growing blank, as if he were sapping her thoughts by some form of witchcraft. She wasn't even aware of what he was saying.

When he put his arms round her, she welcomed them, and as their lips met she accepted it as inevitable. His body was hard next to hers, and deep inside herself she was wishing that they were in bed, with flesh against flesh; nothing separating them. It was how it should be: how it had always been.

How long he held her she didn't know, and it was painful to come back to reality when he released her. She felt as though she were walking through a door leaving Paradise for earthly pain. She said shakily:

" Conan . . . I . . . we mustn't. . . ."

" We have no choice."

" I can't . . . you are married. . . ."

"It makes no difference, and you know it." He caught her wrist, hurting her with the force of his closing fingers. "When you were in my arms, you wanted to be there. Your kiss was as honest as mine. You can't pretend about this, you know that. You've always known it."

He turned abruptly as Crickett appeared in the doorway, letting her hand go. Conan was angry at the interruption, but for once Lalage was glad to see Crickett, murmuring an excuse as she left the butler to deliver his message.

She dared not to go back to her room, for Madge would notice something different about her, and there had to be something different now. She would never be quite the same again, not after that precious but terrible moment in Conan's embrace.

She went to the stables, and the grooms saddled a mare for her. A ride would get rid of the last traces of that hypnotic feeling, which still hadn't quite left her.

She would race as hard as she could, out of the grounds and into the open country, where things were real and pure and reassuring.

She had only ridden a mile or two from Amberstone when she met Gaston Delorme, mounted on his host's new stallion. She reined quickly, glad to see him, for he represented the real world and not a kind of limbo, where there was as much agony as there was pleasure.

He looked even more debonair than usual, his habit immaculate, his smile slightly surprised.

"My dear Lally, wherever are you going at such a pace? Are you running away from Amberstone?"

"No, of course not." She forced herself to keep her tone as light as his. "I just wanted to ride, that's all."

The jewel-bright eyes were searching.

"Or perhaps it was the master of Amberstone from whom you were escaping, eh? Oh, *cherie*, you are blushing, and I have scored a bulls-eye."

"You have done no such thing," she snapped. "How

can you be so absurd, Gaston? Conan Kilmartin is my cousin's husband. What sort of woman do you think I am?"

She was asking the question of herself, as much as of the comte, growing crosser still as he gave a lop-sided grin.

"A very vulnerable one, and most lovely. No wonder Kilmartin turns to you, to get away from that cousin of yours. Any man would."

"May we please change the subject?" She was taut and uncertain of herself in the face of Gaston's comments. "There is nothing between Kilmartin and myself. If you must know why I came riding, it is because I was upset about the death of that poor girl from the village. She hanged herself . . . or so they say."

"Yes, I'd heard." He sobered. "But why do you question the way she died? Don't you think she did kill herself?"

"No." Lalage said it slowly. She hadn't been sure when she'd first heard of Fanny's end, but now she was. "No, I don't. I can't tell you why, but I just don't think she took her own life. The servants say she and the farmer's boy had been. . . ."

"Making love?" Gaston raised an eyebrow. "Why are you so afraid of the word, Lally. You were always blunt enough on the subject in the past."

She ignored the question.

"Very well . . . made love. They say that Roger wasn't going to marry her, and that she couldn't face the shame."

"Well, there's one way to find out."

"How?" She looked up. "The girl's dead, so how can we ask her?"

"Your wits are wandering, my sweet." He was turning his horse's head. "I am not suggesting a sèance to communicate with the dead, but a visit to Priddy's Farm, where I gather her beau works. We can't ask the girl, but we can ask Roger Wheddon what his intentions were."

"You are very well-informed."

" Of course." He waved an airy hand. " Sir James's servants are as garrulous as Kilmartin's. I know all about Fanny, her family, and her beloved. Come, let us go and see him, and put your mind at rest."

When they reached Priddy's Farm, Gaston made himself known to Jack Priddy, stout and bald, and thoroughly irritable because his hands were more interested in some chit's death than in getting his wheat in. However, a few sovereigns soon changed his humour, and he directed Gaston to a field at the south end of the farm.

" Oh yes, I'd be goin' to marry 'er."

Roger Wheddon had a skin burnt nut-brown by the sun, and a mop of bleached hair. His eyes looked watery, and the grief he shewed was clearly genuine.

" I loved 'er," he said simply. " We'd been walkin' out some six months or more. Would 'ave talked to 'er pa, when she were sixteen." The tears welled up again. " Won't never be sixteen now will she?"

" Did she know you were going to marry her?" Gaston was very gentle. " Did you tell her?"

" Of course." Roger brushed an impatient hand across his lashes. Wouldn't do for the gentry to think he was anything but a man, yet he still couldn't get the remembrance of Fanny's face out of his mind. He would never forget it as long as he lived. " We talked of it all the time. Savin' up, we were. Not much, 'o course, for me ma needs most of what I earn 'ere. Still, we'd got a bit put by. She knew right enough, though we'd not named the day."

On the way back to Amberstone, Lalage said sadly:

" I was right. She didn't commit suicide."

" You can't be sure."

" She had no reason."

" You don't know that either. The fact that the lad's intentions were honorable is no proof."

" Why else should she do it?"

" I have no idea. I wasn't in her confidence."

"Really, Gaston!" She was brittle. "I don't think you care a button about that poor child."

He was silent for a moment as they rode along. Then he said:

"I care more about the changes I see in you, Lalage."

"I haven't changed. Don't be silly."

"You most certainly have, although why, I am not yet sure. You are not as you were. You have altered, even since dinner the other night."

She tried not to think about Conan and how she had clung to him, keeping her head high.

"Of course I haven't. Please, Gaston, let it be. Do you think Fanny had been to the folly to see that old woman?"

"Sir James's servants are sure of it. It is because she said Roger was fickle, that she ended her life, or so they would have the world believe."

"But if they were wrong, and Fanny didn't see Nanny Peak." Lalage was talking half to herself. "Then there could have been another explanation for her death. She might have seen something she wasn't meant to."

"Such as the first Mrs. Kilmartin?" He was sceptical. "Come, that's rather unlikely, isn't it?"

"You can scoff, but would you go into that tower at night?"

"Of course," he replied easily, bringing his animal to a halt as they reached the grounds of Amberstone. "Why not? And to assure you that my dissolute life has not impaired either my courage or my intelligence, I will go there to-morrow night. There, does that satisfy you?"

She nodded.

"You'll tell me if you see anything?"

"Naturally."

"Thank you. I must go now."

"Back to your attentive host?" His eyes were half-closed, and the movement of his lips was not even remotely like a smile. "Take care."

" Back to my cousin," she returned coolly, and dug her
heels into the mare's flanks. " And I am always careful, Gaston.
See that you are too."

He watched her go, his face very still, gloved hands clenched
about the reins. He had not thought Lalage would be a problem, but now it seemed that she was. A problem which he
would have to resolve, and in the not too distant future.

He swung round and rode off, not looking back as he raced
madly over the fields towards Watermill, his face dark with
unusual anger.

Five

At eleven-thirty on the following night, Lalage awoke to
Prudence's screams. She had retired early, partly because she
had felt unusually tired after dinner and partly because she
wanted to get away from Conan. He hadn't touched her that
evening: there hadn't been any opportunity for them to be
alone, and she was thankful for it. When she was not with him,
she felt almost like her old self; as she had been, before she
had come to Amberstone. But as soon as she was in a room
with Kilmartin, it was as if some force took control of her.
Then, she was no longer free, or sensible, or even cautious.
She wanted him as much as he obviously wanted her, and it
frightened her.

She dozed for a while, trying to think about Gaston as he
had been as a boy, but the boy had gone. All that was left was
the man who had anger in his eyes when she had ridden away
from him earlier that day. None of his normal gay insouciance,
but a terseness, wholly foreign to him.

When the cries began, Lalage threw the bedclothes back, her thoughts shattered as she groped for her robe. Outside, she found the servants and Madge grouped round Prue, whose whole body was shaking with blind fear.

"Dearest!" Lalage caught Prudence's hand. "What is it? What's wrong?"

"I saw her again." The blank gaze turned to her cousin. "I saw Mercedes, over there, by that stained glass window."

There was a shiver passing through Belinda Isard, Dodo Walsh and Gussie Worboys, whilst Queenie's pinched face was waxen with dread. Lalage was aware that Crickett was sidling up, no flicker of concern visible, and that Una Parkington, clad in a dark grey wrap, was listening to Prudence with compressed lips and a disbelieving air.

"Darling, you couldn't have done." Firmly, Lalage shut out her own quivers. "My love, there's no one by the window."

"Not now, but there was."

"You dreamt it; it was a nightmare."

"No, it wasn't!" The voice was rising in helpless hysteria. "No, I tell you, no! I heard a sound, and when I opened my door and came out on to the landing, there she was. She spoke to me too."

The maids drew back, Worboys beginning to snivel.

"Enough of that, Gussie." Mrs. Parkington was sharp, putting a quick end to the girl's nonsense. "Hold your noise. Can't you see your mistress isn't well?"

"I'm not ill." Prudence gasped the words out, desperate because the ring of faces round her denied her story out of hand. "I tell you she was here. She said I would be the next but one."

Lalage frowned.

"Next but one?"

"Yes, yes." Prue was holding on to Lalage as if without her support she would fall over. "Yes, she said death always came in threes, and I would be the next but one."

Belinda let out a shriek.

" Oh Gawd! Then 'oo's the next?"

" Be quiet, Isard!"

Una again, terse and determined, waving the staff away.

" Go back to your rooms, all of you. Tuesday, make your mistress a hot drink, and be quick about it. Now, madam, let's get you to bed. Won't do for you to stand here like this."

" Where is Mr. Kilmartin?" Reluctantly Lalage surrendered Prue to the housekeeper. " He can't possibly have slept through this."

" Master is out." Crickett was very smooth. " Said he didn't feel tired, and was going for a ride."

" At this time of night?"

" Mr. Kilmartin often rides at night. Now, shall Tuesday get you some milk whilst she's heating the mistress's?"

" Thank you."

Crickett and Una were taking over, and there was nothing that Lalage could do about it. Prue's rigidity had gone, and she was like a limp rag doll as she was led back to her room. Since she could not stand on the landing all night either, Lalage made for her own room.

" Yes, Crickett, I would be grateful, but please call me immediately if Mrs. Kilmartin becomes upset again."

" Of course, Miss, but Mrs. Parkington will see that she gets to sleep. Good night's rest is what she wants."

He padded off, and inside her room, Lalage leaned against the door, making no attempt to get into bed. She was thinking about a half-whisper she had caught as Crickett passed close to Una Parkington. Lalage hadn't heard all of what he had said, but the word ' tower ' had been clear enough. Her brows met wondering what the butler had meant. When the idea came to her, she couldn't throw it off, illogical though it seemed.

Conan had gone to the folly. Why, she hadn't any idea, but she was sure now that she was right. He had gone riding, in the middle of the night, and Crickett had murmured of the tower.

She waited until Tuesday had brought the hot milk, and then

dressed quickly. She realised she was mad to follow Conan on the strength of a smothered remark, but something inside her was urging her on.

She saw the last of the servants' lights disappearing through the green baize door, and then let herself out into the garden. She couldn't find a groom or stable lad: probably they were in the hay loft, snoring their exhaustion away. It didn't matter, for she had learned to ride almost before she had been able to walk, and saddling a mare was no problem.

Walking would take too long: she wanted to catch Kilmartin at *The Ruined Tower*, to find out why he was there. If he wasn't there, she would look an idiot, but no harm would be done, for none had seen her leave.

When she went inside the folly, she held her cloak round her, for even on a warm August night, the tower was as cold as a tomb.

It was also quite empty, and she stood the lantern down on the flat stone, her heart beating faster as she saw the spread Tarot cards. Nanny Peak was about. Lalage couldn't believe the old woman would leave her precious cards unattended for long, and so she called out to her, but Nanny did not reply.

She hesitated, not knowing what to do. She could go back to the house, which was the sensible course to take, or she could wait and see whether the wise woman returned, and whether Conan was with her.

Almost without thinking, she began to pick up the cards, studying them by the light of the lantern. They really were beautiful. Mysterious, crying out to be understood, yet, tantalisingly, shutting themselves off from the uninitiated.

The Magician, with his wide-brimmed hat and his dice, ball and cup on the table in front of him, a wand in his left hand. *La Papesse*, in a simple, graceful robe, the triple tiara on her head, an open book on her lap. *The Lovers*: a young man, with two women from whom he had to choose, a cupid above him, aiming a dart.

Lalage dropped the card of *Death* as the faint noise reached her ears, hastily snuffing out the light and drawing away from the stone.

Pressed against the icy wall, she saw a single candle come into view, moving in her direction. She held her breath, watching as the tiny flame shewed up the outline of the newcomer. Not Nanny Peake: too tall. Conan? She was about to call out to him, when she remembered Gaston Delorme's promise. He had said he would come to the folly that night, to prove that he was neither craven nor witless.

" Gaston, is that you?" She straightened up, laughing shakily. " Good heavens, you frightened the life out of me. I'd forgotten you were coming. Have you seen the wise woman?"

The candle turned towards her again, but there was no reply to her question, and she felt a fresh surge of alarm.

" Gaston! Why don't you answer me? Are you paying me out for doubting you? Oh, very well, I apologise, but for goodness sake speak to me. You're making me nervous."

The figure neither moved nor spoke, and Lalage swallowed hard.

" Gaston! Please!"

The candle went out, and Lalage gasped. She turned to run, but now she had no idea where the opening to the folly was, for it was black as pitch. She blundered on for a few steps, stumbling on the rough ground; then she became aware that someone was very close to her. She could feel their breath; sense a slight movement. Then she screamed.

She was hardly aware of the blow on the head, and certainly knew nothing of the fact that she had sunk unconscious to the floor. The candle was lit again, the figure looking down at her for a few seconds before it moved off and out of the folly.

When Lalage came to, she lay for a while staring into darkness. Her head was throbbing badly, but finally she managed to get up, taking tentative steps, praying that whoever had been there and attacked her, had now gone. It seemed an eternity before she found the door, thankful to feel grass beneath her feet, and to see her mare waiting patiently for her to return.

In the stables, she managed to get the saddle off, her head clearing with the exertion, her mind at last beginning to function again.

She didn't want to think about who had been in the folly. Conan was the obvious choice. Perhaps his anger had spilled over, when he found she had followed him, and he had hit out in rage. Maybe he didn't want to have to explain to her what he was doing there.

Gaston seemed less likely. He had no reason at all to try to harm her, and he couldn't have been unaware that it was she, for she had spoken aloud. No, Gaston wouldn't hurt her, even if he had shewn most unusual anger at their last parting.

She got back into the house through the side door which she had left unlocked. At first, she thought she would wake Madge and tell her all that had happened. Madge would be furious, of course, for well-bred young ladies did not canter about the countryside in the middle of the night, and by now Crickett's whisper seemed a wholly unreasonable excuse for the escapade.

She drank the cup of milk. It was cold, but she needed something to ease the dryness of her throat. When the last drop was gone, she started out for the attics. However cross Madge would be, Lalage needed comfort. A reaction was setting in, and she felt herself on the edge of tears.

Yet when she reached the servants' floor, she stopped again. It wasn't Madge's sort of comfort that she needed, and besides, it was selfish to wake her maid simply because she herself behaved like a fool.

She crossed the landing, meaning to return to her room. Then she saw the second corridor winding away, and almost without thinking she began to follow its path. It was long and narrow, her candle lighting up the cobwebs. Then came a landing and another twist of a passage, and finally a stone arch.

Although she hadn't been near that part of the house before, she knew exactly where she was. A stout oak door barred her way, but beyond it lay the north wing; the place where no one ever went. She waited in silence, holding her breath. Finally she gave a sigh of relief. It had only been an old wives' tale, after all. There was nothing up here but dust and the faint scuffle of a mouse behind the wainscotting.

She was turning away, feeling much better now that at last one rumour had proved to be false, when she heard it. She swung round quickly, raising the candle to stare at the solid door.

The sound, whatever it was, was growing louder. It was as if there was some kind of animal behind the wood, crouched low, waiting to get out. Yet instinct told her it wasn't an ordinary animal. It wasn't a growl nor yet a snarl, but something in between: furthermore, the creature must have had strong talons, for she could hear violent scratching of wood.

She began to back away, limbs like lead. Whatever it was, beast or human, it wasn't a ghost. It was very real; very alive. Frantically clawing to get out; desperate to get at her throat.

How she got back to the main part of the house, she didn't know. Endless passages and stairs, all muddled up, fear making her take wrong turnings. Finally, she got to the second floor landing, pausing to hold on to the banister, trying to compose herself.

She wondered if she would have enough courage in the morning to ask Kilmartin what it was. She shivered, knowing she wouldn't dare. In any event, there was no way in which she could explain what she had been doing up in that dark and awful place. In any event, she didn't really want to know what it was. It was better left buried.

"Lalage?"

She moaned, and nearly dropped the candle, scarcely realising that Kilmartin had taken it from her, and was setting it down on a small side table.

"What is it?"

"Oh . . . Conan! You frightened me. I thought it was . . ."

"Yes?"

Now was the moment to tell him what she had heard, if ever she were going to tell him, but she let the second pass.

"It's nothing. Prudence was upset earlier on. I wanted to be sure that she was all right."

"She is; I've just looked in. She's sleeping soundly, but her nightmare was more than three hours ago, I understand. Surely you haven't been awake since then?"

She tried not to look guilty. If it had been he in the folly, he would be suspicious. She bluffed it out.

"Oh no. I roused, and thought about Prue. I hated to see her so frightened."

"Kind Lalage." He tilted her chin. "But then you are kind, aren't you? Your concern for my wife is most touching."

"Are you laughing at me?"

"Only in the gentlest of ways."

"I doubt if you could be gentle."

"You do me an injustice. I can be as gentle as a dove, at times."

"I hadn't noticed it."

"Hadn't you? You must have forgotten."

His first kiss was so delicate that she hardly felt it, his arm slipped round her waist to support her, and to hold her closer to him.

She wanted to look away, but it was impossible. It was as if he were forcing her to remain still as he bent his head again.

"Don't . . . Conan . . . don't. It's wrong, you know it is."

"Come to my room."

"No, no! I can't!"

"No one will see us. I've told you, Amberstone keeps its secrets."

"You're Prudence's husband."

" And bitterly does she regret it."

" My aunt says you bought her."

" Does she now?" He was smiling. " Perhaps I did. I needed a wife when Mercedes died. I wanted a son."

" And now you have one."

She fought back, seizing her weapon quickly before it could elude her.

" Let's go and see him, Conan. Let us go to the nursery, and see Denzil. I would like that."

She watched the change come over him, as if a mask had been torn off, leaving another man's face beneath it for the world to see.

" No." He was curt, his arm dropping to his side. " The child's asleep: it's nearly three o'clock."

" We needn't wake him." She had the upper hand now, triumphant because at last she had succeeded in shaking off the feelings he seemed to be able to arouse in her so easily. " Come, I'll lead the way. It's on the third floor, isn't it?"

His hand was like a vice, forcing her back, his face white with temper.

" No! I have said no. Let that be enough."

" Such mystery!" She taunted him. " Another of Amberstone's secrets?"

When he struck her, she gave a cry, one hand covering her bruised cheek. She knew that she deserved it, but she hadn't thought Conan would hit her. She was stupid to imagine that his desire to make love to her would protect her from his wrath.

They stood there for another long second, Conan's mouth like a trap, Lalage shrinking back. Then he gave a deep sigh, as if he were coming back from a long way off.

" I shouldn't have done that."

Slowly the fear seeped out of her; she was safe again. Conan's passion was spent.

" No, it's my fault," she whispered. " You were right, it's too late to see Denzil to-night."

She was meek, letting him believe that the hour was her only reason for giving in. She would have to wait for another opportunity to find out where Prue's son really was, and why his cot was occupied by a doll. Now was not the moment.

He stroked her face where the blow had fallen.

"Beloved, did I hurt you?"

She could feel the weakness beginning again, trying to edge away.

"No, no, it was nothing. It doesn't matter."

"To me it does."

"I must go. It's very late, as you say."

She knew that was the moment when she should have turned and ran, but she didn't move.

"Is it convention, I wonder, or lack of courage?"

"I have no idea what you mean."

"You know." He laughed at her pretence, his arm round her again. "You know perfectly well what I'm talking about. Well, which is it?"

She was trembling now because he was so close to her. It was as if she no longer belonged to herself, but was a part of him, and it was an effort to get the words out.

"I don't think I'm a coward."

"No, you were never that."

She made one last attempt.

"Conan, let me go. I don't understand what is happening to me." She tried to pull away from him. "I only know that I must go."

It was too late. His hold on her had tightened, one hand slipped into the neck of her robe, strong fingers moving intimately down her throat towards her breast. She no longer tried to stop him; the feeling was a wonderful one. Every part of her seemed unusually alive; there was a vivid awareness of her own body which she had never experienced before. Just fleetingly she wondered if she were right about that. Somewhere deep in her mind, she felt that she had known

D

ecstasy like this long ago. It didn't matter: the present was what counted.

After a moment he said:

"Your skin is like silk, my love. So smooth, so white."

"Conan."

It wasn't a plea any longer, nor a protestation. She wanted his hands on her, not just on her neck, but all over her, exultant when he slipped the peignoir from one shoulder. She was in her other world once more; the world in which she and Conan could be lovers, and where time stood still whilst they embraced and held each other.

As he lifted her in his arms and started for the stairs, she lay passive against him. Soon, she would be his again. A few stairs and a foot or two of passage were all which separated them from complete fulfilment; from something which was theirs of right.

When they heard footsteps, Conan swore under his breath, and Lalage was jerked back to sanity. Kilmartin had let her go, and she stood by his side, holding the wrap tightly about her.

"Sorry, sir." Crickett was smug, his regret as false as his words. "Thought I heard a sound."

"You did." Kilmartin was in complete control of himself. "Miss Ashmore was just coming down to make sure that my wife was all right. Go to bed, Crickett."

The butler sidled off, and Lalage knew that he would be grinning. She gave an unhappy laugh. All the magic was gone, and only the shame was left.

"It seems it is not to be. I shouldn't have . . ."

"Not this time, perhaps, but eventually it will happen. You know it has to."

"No! It can't! Good-night, Conan."

She got into bed, almost too exhausted to sleep. Her mind was a jumble of thoughts and unanswered questions about the north wing, the attacker in the folly, and most of all, Conan, and the way she responded to him.

After a while, she couldn't understand at all why she had wanted him. The hunger for him, or whatever it was, had disappeared so completely that she felt nothing but astonishment at her own behaviour. Then that went too, and she could scarcely remember what had passed between them, convincing herself that they had merely met on the landing and exchanged a few words.

Her eyes filled with tears, and she wanted to talk to someone who would understand, and not think her mad. She didn't know why Gaston sprang into her mind, nor why she felt an urgent need to hold his hand and unburden her troubles.

She could see him, with his bright, shrewd eyes and slow, tolerant smile; his inner strength, and sure self-possession.

She turned her head into the pillow and began to cry. What on earth was wrong with her? Was Amberstone making her as strange as Prue? One minute longing for Delorme, the next thinking about Prue's husband.

But soon the misery was done as fatigue got its own way. Whatever was the matter with her, she was too tired to think about it any more that night. Lalage turned on her side and fell into a deep sleep.

* * *

When Lalage took her place at the table next morning, Conan inclined his head politely as he rose. It was a formal gesture, as if she were an ordinary guest in his house whom he saw only now and then. She was glad; it was how it should be. Prudence was withdrawn as usual, paying no attention to her food or to her husband and cousin.

Lalage had woken that day determined to fight against whatever it was that Conan did to her. It wouldn't be easy, because it was such an intangible thing, taking a form that seemed more like an illusion than anything else. He was strong but she would have to be stronger still. She would have to

ensure that they were never alone again, for it was only then
that it happened. She said lightly:

"Did you sleep well, Conan? I did, once I knew Prue was
all right."

She waited for his reaction: a look which would confirm or
deny what she believed might have occurred. There was
nothing: he went on buttering his toast.

"Very well thank you."

"Isn't it a beautiful morning." She wasn't put down by his
coolness. "I shall go for a long walk, I think. There is so much
to see at Amberstone. How long has it been in your family?"

"Almost three hundred years."

"So long?" She sipped strong black coffee, her smile impersonal. "What would happen if there were no heir?"

He paused fractionally, knife stilled.

"There always has been one."

"So far, yes, but what if you hadn't got a son? Who would
get Amberstone?"

He didn't like the turn of the conversation, his tone bleak.

"It would pass to the female line, but that is hardly likely
to occur is it?"

"No, of course not. You have Denzil, haven't you? I'm so
longing to see him."

Their eyes met: hers innocent, his like flints, both ignoring
Prue's unhappy whimper.

"Soon, perhaps."

"Who is the heir-presumptive, or perhaps I should say,
heiress-presumptive? To whom would Amberstone pass, if
Denzil did not exist?"

He sat back in his chair, Prudence tearing at her napkin,
waiting for him to answer. Lalage could see the tension in
him; the ugly line of his mouth.

"If you must persist in this somewhat pointless conversation, I will satisfy your thirst for knowledge if only to silence
your incessant questions at this hour of the morning. It would
pass to a woman called Dominica Travers, at least, that was

her maiden name. I believe she married: a foreigner, I think."

Lalage's hands began to shake and she hid them quickly in her lap, thankful for once that Crickett was hovering, filling his master's cup. Perhaps Conan was watching him, and hadn't noticed that her colour had flown and all her fierce intention to fight him, in any way she could, had gone with it.

Finally her voice was steady enough to speak.

" Yes, that's right. She married a Frenchman. His name was Delorme, and he died two years ago. His son is now the Comte de Lys. You know Gaston, of course. Dominica Travers is his mother."

Six

As Lalage got ready to go riding with Prue, she was very silent. Conan's words had shaken her world to its foundations, although why the thought of Gaston had suddenly become so important to her, she still did not know. It was all part of the madness which had struck at her since she came to Foxcove.

The possibilities stemming from Conan's pronouncement were profoundly disturbing, making her sick at heart.

Gaston must have known his mother would inherit Amberstone, should Kilmartin fail to have an heir. Was that why he had come to stay at Watermill, to make sure the son Prue had borne did not survive? And, if he were that ruthless, was it, after all, he who had struck her down in the folly?

She looked at herself in the mirror, half expecting to see two reflections, for she felt like two women. One, a wanton, almost in love with Prue's husband, the other a girl who had light-

heartedly flirted with many young blades, having no intention
of taking any of them seriously, and now, too late, recognised
that her feelings for Gaston were a good deal deeper than she
had realised.

It was as if she were possessed: as if her body had been taken
over, slipping from her control. She wished Aunt Ann were
there, so that she could talk to her. Old she might have been,
but she was worldly-wise, and would help. It was no use going
to Madge: she would merely wring her hands and demand
they return to London.

Of course that was what they should do, but Lalage knew
she couldn't leave. Whatever the ties were which held her,
they were strong and binding.

Other nasty thoughts crowded in on her. Why was there a
doll in Denzil's cot? Was it possible that there was no son:
that Prue's child had been stillborn? Conan might be trying to
fool his staff and his friends, concealing the truth, even from
Prue herself. Perhaps Gaston was setting out to call his
bluff.

The reflection in the glass was just what she had always
seen: there was no sign of what was splitting her in
half like a rotten apple, and she turned away quickly. Perhaps if she stood there too long, she would see something
which would drive her to Prue's kind of mental instability

Her cousin was waiting for her when she got to the drive,
looking less scared now and almost attractive in her dark blue
habit with a crimson scarf at her neck. Lalage wondered
whether to try to talk to Prue, now she seemed calmer, but
her hesitation was too long. Prue was already beginning to
canter off, and Lalage had no choice but to follow. They
had just got beyond the grounds, when Prue called out.

"Look, there are Sir James and Lucinda, and isn't that
Gaston with them?"

Lalage stiffened in the saddle. The last person she wanted to
meet just then was Delorme, but the others had already seen
them, and were riding towards them.

Lalage concentrated on Sir James, having no idea what they were talking about, keenly aware of the comte smiling gently at Prudence.

The moment couldn't be put off for ever, and when Prue moved on to speak to the Lauries, Gaston urged his mount nearer.

"Well, and how are you to-day?"

He took in the troubled hazel eyes, the droop of the lovely mouth. He had forgotten what a beauty she was, this girl he had known for so long. She was so much more mature than he had remembered her, as if she understood what life was all about. The thought did not sit easily with him, and he said musingly:

"You do not answer. Does that mean that you are unwell?"

"No, no, of course not." She was evasive, not looking at him. "I'm perfectly all right. Don't fuss, Gaston."

"I hardly think I was doing that."

She didn't say anything, and he tried again.

"Will you ride with me to-morrow?"

"Perhaps. I shall have to see."

"You are so heavily engaged?"

The thin eyebrows rose in surprise, and she looked uncomfortable.

"No, it's not that. I just don't know what I'll be doing to-morrow. Please excuse me, I must go and speak to Sir James."

"That you have done." He was short with her. "Why are you trying to avoid me?"

"I'm not. What an absurd notion. Really, Gaston, you are becoming quite a bore."

There was nothing he could do. He watched Lalage and Prue bid the Lauries good-bye, seeing the urgency with which Lalage raced off. The tiger eyes were hard. She was suspicious; that was obvious. How much she knew, or guessed, he didn't know, but he would have to find out quickly, before it was too late.

*   *   *

After dinner that night, Lalage pleaded a headache and retired to her room, but she didn't stay there. She didn't want to go to the folly again, for the place was eerie and frightening, but she had to see Nanny Peak. She knew she was being a fool, yet the old woman seemed to know so much. Perhaps she could explain some of the things which were taking place.

She had refused to glance in Conan's direction during the meal, studiedly ignoring him, except when she was forced to answer a direct question. She could sense his anger, but she wouldn't give in. She had to keep away from him.

Madge was in her bedroom with an upset stomach, and it was easier for Lalage to slip out of the house without anyone noticing. The night was warm and there was a moon, but as she approached *The Ruined Tower*, Lalage could feel the knot inside herself tightening. When she stood in front of it, she hesitated. There was still time to go back to the house; she didn't have to go in.

Finally she overcame the momentary weakness, and then she was inside, seeing Nanny Peak in her usual place, the Tarot cards laid out before her.

" Thought you'd come back," she said, when Lalage came within the light of the lamp perched on the stone. " Knew you were an inquisitive one, first time I saw you. Well, what do you want now?"

" I'm not sure." Lalage tried to see beyond the shadows, but it was impossible. Only the hands were visible, moving the cards with swift, sure precision. " Strange things are going on, and I don't know what to do."

The old woman laughed.

" Aye, it's because of Amberstone, of course. Touches everyone who lives in it."

" But I'm only staying there, and the things I mean . . . at least some of them . . . don't seem to have anything to do with the house itself."

The cards flicked over.

"Everything's to do with it, mark my words. Well, what's troubling you? That cousin of yours?"

"Partly. She wants to see her baby, and they won't let her."

"Just as well."

"Why do you say that? Is there something wrong with him?"

Four more cards turned face up, hands fluttering over them.

"Best you don't know."

"But I want to know."

"Well, you won't. What else?"

This time, Lalage's hesitation was longer. She wasn't sure that she could trust the woman, and Nanny was far from sympathetic. What if she spoke of the confidences she, Lalage, was considering imparting. As if the wise woman could read her thoughts, Nanny said softly:

"Say what you want to. No one else will ever know. Give me your half-sovereign, and speak your mind. Your secrets are safe with me."

"Oh yes, of course."

Hastily Lalage paid her dues.

"Good, now what troubles you, my pretty one? Not just that wishy-washy girl, I'll be bound. More than that, isn't it?"

"Yes, but I don't know how to explain."

"Not hard, once you start."

"Well, it is really. It's most extraordinary, and I'm sure you'll think I'm feeble minded."

"Maybe I won't."

"Well, you see . . ." Lalage took a deep breath, feeling as if she were stripping herself bare. "It's when I'm with Mr. Kilmartin that. . . ."

"Yes?"

The cards kept moving, but there was a quickened interest in the voice.

" I feel . . . that is . . . I believe . . . I think I've known him before."

Silence; just steady breathing, the old woman waiting.

" I know it's absurd, but the feeling is so strong. There are times, after we've been together, when I can't remember what we said to each other or what happened, yet I'm sure that something did. And I want him to. . . ."

" Go on."

" I . . . can't! I can't put it into words."

" Yes you can." The fingers were finally stilled, the whisper ragged now. " Want him to what?"

" Make love to me."

It was out at last, and suddenly the remembrance of her night meeting with Conan was as clear as if it were happening there and then Her throat was dry, in spite of the extra cups of coffee she had had after dinner; so dry that she could hardly swallow, and she felt almost light-headed.

She was shaking a little, partly with shame, but partly with the sheer relief of being able to put it into words to another human being, even the old wise woman, yet she couldn't leave it there. She had to explain.

" I don't really want him to." She took a step forward and was promptly waved back. " I wouldn't try to take my own cousin's husband from her, but when I am with him, it is as though I don't belong to myself any more. As if I am a different person altogether. I can't remember either. I'm not certain whether things have happened, or whether I've dreamt them. And there's another thing. . . ."

Her voice trailed off, and the old woman snapped at her.

" Go on, girl, go on."

Lalage shut her eyes. She hadn't thought Nanny would pass moral judgements, but the disapproval was obvious, and she had made a fatal mistake in coming to the folly.

" The Comte de Lys is here."

" So I've heard. What of it?"

" I've known him since I was a child, and I thought I had no deep feelings for him. I was fond of him, of course, but now . . . We haven't seen one another for the last year or two, and I imagined that it would be as it was before. He was like a brother."

" Now you're not so sure?"

The cackle was scornful.

" No, I'm not. It is a terrible feeling, and I know that I can't make you understand. I don't know why I came really." Her voice was low. " It was a stupid thing to have done. You can't tell me whether I'm sane or not."

Lalage could feel tears on her cheeks. How could she have said so much to a dirty old woman? Where was her dignity; her pride? But it was too late now, and she said drearily:

" I can't love two men at the same time. It isn't possible . . . it's unnatural, and I'm frightened."

" Has he made love to you?"

" Gaston? Oh no, he wouldn't."

" No, not him. The other one. Conan Kilmartin."

" No . . . no."

" You don't sound sure about it." The whisper was as sour as a lemon. " Tell me the whole truth, if you want my help. Lies won't do you any good now."

" No, I know. Well, we might have made love, but we were interrupted." The folly seemed to fade for a second, and she was in Conan's arms again. Just as abruptly, the image faded. " I don't expect you to believe me, but I was glad. I should have been no better than a common whore, but I know that I couldn't have stopped him. I just . . . don't know what to do."

" Go home."

" I can't. There's Prue, you see."

" Lie to yourself, but not to me."

" I'm not!"

" Yes you are. You want them both, don't you? Kilmartin

and this other man. Well, you won't get them. Maybe you won't get either, for neither of them is what you believe him to be."

Lalage's heart sank. She knew Nanny Peak was right, but it hurt to hear the blunt truth.

" I'll tell you this, though. One of them means you harm."

" Which one?"

" Can't tell yet, but one of them will kill you if he gets the chance."

" What shall I do?" Lalage felt stunned, her own will sapped as she put herself into the hands of Nanny Peak. Her throat was drier still, a bitter taste on her tongue. " I'll do whatever you advise, except that I can't go back to London yet."

" First, I'll give you one of my specials to make you sleep. See, over there on that shelf. Drink it up, all of it; then we'll see. I'll think about it, and when you come again, I'll tell you what to do. Meanwhile, keep away from Kilmartin."

" You think he's the one?"

" I've told you; I don't know yet. Just keep away from him. Now be off with you; I'm tired."

When Lalage returned to the house, she felt worse than ever. She had forgotten to ask Nanny about other things, such as the doll, and the north wing. All she had done was to confess herself a harlot to a grubby old crone who sat in the folly reading fortunes.

She drank the contents of the phial nevertheless. Whatever it was, it couldn't make her feel worse, and perhaps it might make her sleep. She threw the container into some bushes and went in through the side door.

The stairs seemed to waver as she went up to her room, and she had to hold on to the banister to stop herself from falling.

" Lalage."

She shrank back as Conan moved out of the shadows on the second floor landing.

" You're up very late. I thought you had a headache."

"I . . . I . . . did. I hoped some air . . ."

"I see."

She wanted to push past him, but whatever the wise woman had given her was making her muzzy, eyes not able to focus properly.

"I . . . I . . . must go . . . to bed."

"Yes, of course."

His hands were gentle yet firm; a well-remembered and habitual caress.

"No . . . no . . ."

She knew his mouth was over hers, and that she could feel the beat of his heart against hers, but she couldn't fight him off. He was too powerful, and she had no resistance left. The world was tilting crazily, and she felt sick and giddy. As the blackness closed in, she was aware that he had caught her in his arms as she fell. After that, there was nothing.

*   *   *

The next evening they dined with Colonel Philpot and his wife, Cressida. Lalage had woken that morning with very little recollection of what had happened the night before. She knew that she had been to the folly, but what Nanny Peak had said to her, she could hardly remember. Somewhere, tucked well away in the back of her mind, she had the feeling that upon her return to the house, she had met Conan, but she wasn't sure. It was just a vague impression, and she didn't want to think about it. Probably it had been a dream, no more.

She was not pleased to find Gaston there, with Sir James and Lady Laurie, thankful that her place at table was too far away from him for conversation to be possible. After the meal was over, she took refuge in the conservatory, but her solitude didn't last for long. Gaston strolled in, taking a seat opposite her, ignoring her heightened colour.

"Do you know, Lalage," he said finally. "I am beginning

to believe you really are going out of your way to avoid me, despite what you said the other morning."

She opened her fan, cooling her cheeks with quick, fluttering movements.

"Why should I do that?"

"I hoped you would tell me."

"It is your imagination."

"I think not. What on earth is the matter with you, Lally? One would almost think you were afraid of me."

His normal bantering tone was gone, and one slim, strong hand had closed hard over her wrist.

"Gaston! Let me go; you're hurting me."

The grip didn't slacken.

"Answer me! Why won't you talk to me? What's wrong?"

"Nothing! I've told you; nothing! Now please let me go."

"Very well."

Slowly his fingers relaxed, but his lips were as tight as ever.

She couldn't bring herself to look at him, but she said in a small voice:

"Were you at the folly that night? The night you said you were going."

There was a pause, and finally she had to turn her head.

"No." His eyes were unreadable, like holes in a mask. "No, I wasn't. I was unavoidably detained, but I haven't forgotten my promise."

"Are you sure you weren't there?"

"Quite sure." He flicked ash from his cigar. "It is hardly the kind of thing one is likely to forget, is it? Now, if you say there is nothing wrong between us, kiss me, to shew that we are still friends."

"No! Not here."

"Why ever not? We are alone."

He saw her shudder, his expression growing savage.

"Kiss me, Lalage!"

She started uneasily at his tone. It was a peremptory order, not an entreaty from an old friend.

She turned away, hoping that he would merely give her a peck, but he jerked her back and held her so tightly that she could hardly breathe. His mouth bruised hers, as if he hated her, and was punishing her.

When he let her go, she was white and shaken. Gaston had never behaved like that before. She was about to speak, when she looked past him, her eyes darkening.

Conan was standing in the doorway of the conservatory. For a brief moment it was as if they were alone: then he moved away, and Gaston said softly:

"Let him see, my dear. What does it matter? The sooner he realises that you are not for him the better."

*   *   *

When Lalage went to see Madge the next morning, her maid was still poorly, propped up in bed, face like bleached calico.

"Oh, Madge!"

Lalage was conscience-stricken. She had been so preoccupied by her own affairs, that she had hardly thought about Madge.

"I'll be all right." Madge was weak; just talking was an effort. "They're looking after me well. Even that Tuesday wench has been bringing me plenty of warm drinks. Stupid to get like this; can't think what's wrong with me."

"I'll get a doctor."

"Goodness me, you won't." Briefly, Madge was her old aggressive self. "Just got the collywobbles, that's all. Be up and about before you know it."

"Are you sure?"

"Quite."

The older woman looked at her mistress for a long while. Then she said:

"Glad you've come, though. Wanted to talk to you."

Immediately, Lalage was on her guard.

"Oh yes? What about?"

"You know what about."

"I don't. How could I?"

The haughty tone gained Lalage nothing.

"Oh yes you do, my girl. I may have the stomach-ache, but my brains are not addled, nor am I deaf to the gossip that's going on about you and Mr. Conan."

"Gossip?" Lalage tensed. "What gossip? I haven't heard anything."

"Well, of course you haven't." Madge was tart. "You'd be the last one to hear, wouldn't you? But I have. All the servants are gabbing about the way you look at him. You ought to be thoroughly ashamed of yourself, brought up properly like you were, and your own cousin's husband into the bargain. Whatever are you thinking about?"

Lalage was on the point of spitting back, reminding Madge that it was none of her business, when suddenly she buried her head in her hands, her voice unsteady.

"I know, I know, and I am ashamed, but I can't help it. Oh God, if you only knew! I really can't help it. It's what he does to me; I don't know how. I just know that when he's near me. I can't . . ."

"Nothing's happened, has it?"

Madge's breath was drawn in sharply, and Lalage shook her head, thrusting down the thought of that night when she had fainted in Conan's arms. How could she be sure what had happened after that?

"No, no."

"Praise God for that. We must go home." Madge was trying to sit up, the effort too much for her. "Miss Lalage, we must go."

"We can't . . . Prue . . . I can't leave her."

Madge sank back against the pillows, her eyes closing wearily.

"Can't leave him, you mean. He'll ruin you, see if he doesn't. What the comte will say when he hears, I dare not think."

Lalage shrank inside herself. She couldn't talk to Madge

about Gaston, and how he had changed. She could still feel the pressure of his kiss on her lips, as if he had had nothing but contempt for her. Whatever happened, Madge mustn't find out about that, or who would inherit Amberstone, if Conan had no heir.

"And there's another thing." Madge's voice was growing tired, but clear enough for every syllable to be heard. "We've been here more than a week now, and I haven't heard as much as a single cry from that baby, have you?"

Not a subject which Lalage wanted to discuss, but it was better than thinking of Gaston.

"No, I haven't, but some of them sleep a lot."

"Never known an infant that quiet, but if he isn't making a noise, something else is."

Lalage could feel her heart begin to thump.

"Oh?"

"Didn't mean to tell you this, but the morning I was taken bad, I went up to the attics, looking for that girl, Tuesday. Lost my way, I suppose, for I found myself over on the north side."

"The north wing?"

Lalage was hardly breathing, hands gripped tightly together.

"That's right. There was a door; great stout thing. Take it from me, there's something behind it; something downright unnatural. Oh, Miss Lalage, don't, don't. Oh, poppet, don't!"

It was too late. Lalage had dissolved into tears.

*   *   *

Lalage was sitting in the garden-room, trying to read and stifle dreadful thoughts. It was four o'clock, and soon Isard would be bringing in the tea; tiny sandwiches, wafer thin, and sugared cakes with cherries on the top.

Her tears were done, but her worries weren't. Madge's experience in the north wing had awoken all the old fears of the curse said to be laid upon the Kilmartins, but now the dread was mixed with the feelings she had for Conan. The fact that the servants were talking about her and Conan was humiliating, yet somehow it didn't seem to matter any more. Amberstone kept its secrets, so Conan had said, and it put up a barrier between itself and the real world outside. Let the staff chatter if they wanted to.

The door opened and Lalage turned eagerly, hoping it was Kilmartin, but it wasn't. It was Prue, looking so different that Lalage stared at her in blank amazement. There was wild-rose in her cousin's cheeks, the blue eyes alight. She recognised the riding habit as one of her own: Prue must have borrowed it without saying a word. It fitted her perfectly, emphasizing the waist, the jacket giving her curves she didn't really possess.

"I've been riding," she said, and threw her hat on to the sofa. "Oh, Lalage, it was wonderful, wonderful!"

She saw Lalage's astonishment and giggled.

"Well, why shouldn't I go riding? It's a perfect afternoon, we had such fun."

"We? You mean Conan went with you?"

"Good heavens, no!" Prue went over to the mirror by the window, admiring herself, touching her face, as if she were seeing herself for the first time. "No, I was with Gaston. He rides magnificently, and he's very good-looking, don't you think?"

Lalage felt as though Prue had stabbed her. It was another sensation she had never had before, but she recognised it at once. It was jealousy. She almost laughed aloud, but there was no humour in the situation. She, Lalage, who wanted Prue's husband to make love to her, jealous because her cousin had gone riding with Gaston. It was totally ridiculous, and she pulled herself together quickly.

"Yes, isn't he?" Light and casual; no great interest shewn. "Where did you go?"

"Oh, I don't know . . . everywhere." Prue was still smiling at herself in the glass. "I know that we went near the old quarry, for I nearly slipped down it."

Lalage turned sharply.

"Slipped? What do you mean?"

"Just that. I almost fell."

"And Gaston saved you?"

"No, he didn't notice what had happened. We'd got off the horses and were walking. He must have been looking elsewhere." Prue came away from the mirror, still light-hearted. "Do you know, it was almost as if someone had pushed me, but that couldn't have been, of course, because only Gaston was there. I shall go and change before tea. Oh, I don't know when I was last as happy as I am now."

Lalage watched the door close. She wanted to scream at Prue and warn her to watch Gaston. Her cousin was an innocent, and she was obviously unaware of the connection between Amberstone and the comte.

Prue had said: 'It was almost as if someone had pushed me'. Lalage shivered. Perhaps they had. If de Lys had believed Prudence's child was stillborn, he might have tried to ensure that she did not conceive again.

"Oh God!"

Lalage whispered the words aloud, feeling the weight of tears behind her eyes. It wasn't only the dread of what Gaston might do which made her die a little inside. She hated Prue for looking so happy after an hour or two with Delorme.

She went to the mirror which Prue had used, assessing herself cold-bloodedly. What had happened to the assured Miss Ashmore, whose emotions were always under iron control? The civilised Miss Ashmore, who had never experienced jealousy or passion before, and whose approach to life had been prosaic and very matter-of-fact.

"She's dead."

This time she didn't say it out loud, but to herself. The girl she had been, not much more than a week ago, no longer existed. Now another being lived inside her body and controlled her mind. A strange, fey creature who thought she recognised things she could never have seen before; an idiot, who went to a so-called witch for advice, and imagined herself to be in love with two men at the same time.

She couldn't face having tea with Prue, and so she went up to her room, thankful to be alone. Madge was making good progress, but she wouldn't be up until the next day. For the moment, Lalage had the blessing of privacy.

She felt hot and sticky, for the garden-room was very warm for a day like that. Too much glass, sucking in the sun, making the plants grow high, but shrivelling humans.

There was cold water in the painted jug on the washstand; scented soap next to the bowl. In another minute, she was tugging her clothes off, splashing water recklessly, as if to wash away all the badness which had occurred since she had arrived. She was so engrossed in what she was doing, that she didn't hear the door open, and gave an exclamation as Tuesday said chirpily:

"Here you are, Miss. Thought you'd like a glass of lemon, seein' it's such a scorcher."

Lalage put her robe on quickly, and Sabrina tittered.

"No call to do that 'cos of me. Seen enough women in the altogether in me time."

"Yes, of course."

The girl made Lalage feel uncomfortable and a prude; like a country bumpkin.

"Thank you, Tuesday, that was kind of you."

The maid shewed no sign of going, beady eyes on Lalage's body under the thin wrap.

"Drink it up, Miss. Mrs. Nuttall's best, that is."

It seemed the quickest way of getting rid of Sabrina, so Lalage drank the contents of the glass. It was icy cold, with a touch of something almost spicy mixed with the fruit.

"Delicious." Lalage had regained her composure, deciding that the girl shouldn't get everything her own way. A few awkward questions might put the maid out of countenance too. "Tell me, since you know so much of what goes on here: what is this tale I hear about the north wing?"

The smirk died, and Tuesday began to make for the door.

"Nothin' that I know of. Just empty rooms over there."

"That's not what I've been told."

A shrug, one hand on the knob.

"Well, you know how it is, Miss. Them girls downstairs love to chatter."

"I think there's more to it than that. Tell me . . ."

But Sabrina had gone, the door shut fast. Lalage began to dry herself, deep in thought. That had really scared the girl; she wouldn't even talk about the matter.

Lalage sighed. She would try again later, but now a peculiar weariness was overcoming her. She had meant to go out again, but suddenly the bed was drawing her to it, the thought of a nap too enticing to forego. She found a dry robe and lay down, eyelids drooping as if fingers were forcing them shut.

She had no idea how much time had passed when she heard the door open again: it could have been minutes or hours. She just knew that there were steps crossing the floor to the bed, drowsy as she tried in vain to open her eyes.

"Conan? Is that you?"

She didn't know why she asked that, nor why she hoped her guess was right. She had promised herself never again to be alone with him, but now she was smiling as she felt familiar hands on her.

"Conan? Why don't you answer?"

There was still no reply, and the weights on her eyelids were too heavy for her to see for herself. She simply knew that the grip on her hand had tightened, and that she was being raised from the pillow, held against another body, whose warmth she could feel through the flimsy wrap.

When she finally awoke, it was a quarter to eight. She got off the bed quickly, feeling as if she had been drunk. She couldn't remember lying down, nor did she understand why she had undressed. There was the faintest recollection that someone had touched her, but it blew away too rapidly for her to hold on to.

Somehow she managed to get herself ready by eight o'clock, admirably composed as she joined Prue. Prudence was in a loose grey frock, hair escaping in wisps. All the prettiness and joy of the afternoon had gone so completely that Lalage began to wonder whether she had imagined how her cousin had looked when she returned from her ride.

She felt a twinge of real nervousness. Always so sure of herself, her present state was totally unnerving. She was beginning to imagine things; not certain whether events were real, or if she had been dreaming. Is that what Amberstone had done to Prue? She looked at her cousin with new eyes, recognising that hitherto she had been somewhat critical. Now, such thoughts were washed away in the certain knowledge that there was a force at work in Conan's house which was stronger than human will.

They were waiting in the sitting-room, and since there was no sign of Conan, and Prue was clearly in no mood for conversation, Lalage went round the room glancing at the paintings. She avoided the one of Mercedes, concentrating on the landscapes and pictures of flowers, until suddenly she stopped dead.

Near the window, above a small table, there was a portrait in an oval gold frame, and Lalage could feel herself growing cold. The woman in the picture was so like herself, it was as if she were staring into a mirror. The hair, the eyes, the skin, the mouth: they were exactly like her own. She said tautly:

" Prue, this painting. Who is it?"

Prudence didn't answer. She seemed far away, as if in a different place.

" Prue! Listen to me! Who is it?"

Still no answer, and then Crickett was there, announcing dinner, and she had to let the matter drop.

When she found no sign of Kilmartin in the dining-room, her heart missed another beat.

" Where is Mr. Kilmartin, Crickett?"

Crickett served the soup carefully, Belinda in the background.

" Not back from Oxford, Miss. Been there all day. I expect the storm delayed him."

" Storm?"

Lalage's spoon shook in her hand. She had no recollection of a storm, but then, of course, she had been asleep. An uneasy nap, which had left a queer aftermath.

" I didn't know we'd had a storm. It must have been while I was resting."

The butler's mouth curved in a smile which Lalage didn't like.

" Possibly, Miss, though the thunder was loud enough to wake the dead."

He was gone, and Lalage forced herself to taste the soup. It was very good, but she wasn't hungry, and there was the same dry, bitterness in her mouth. She longed for the meal to be over, so that she could be by herself and think.

Could she really have slept through a storm as noisy as Crickett had described it? It hadn't seemed like a normal sleep from the beginning. No recollection of lying down: odd flashes of memory, too intangible to capture and examine: the feel of hands moving over her body. But Conan was in Oxford: he'd been there all day.

And now the picture of a woman who looked exactly as she, Lalage, looked, wearing a dress which would have been fashionable a century before. When the butler came back with the next course, she wondered whether to ask him about it, but she couldn't find the right words.

She and Prue had coffee in the sitting-room, Lalage keeping well away from the window. She was beginning to feel a little better, food and strong coffee forcing her mind to work normally again. There was nothing so extraordinary about finding a painting of a woman who looked like her. Doubles weren't unknown, and probably if she got up to have another look at the portrait, she would find it wasn't nearly so close a resemblance as she had first thought. It was just another trick of the mind.

Her confidence lasted until Prue had gone, and she got back to her bedroom. Conan hadn't returned, and the house was very quiet. She undressed, brushing her hair slowly to while away the time. She would be glad when to-morrow came, and Madge was up. Even if she nagged, she was someone to talk to.

Then she went to the bed again, feeling tired once more. She couldn't understand the lethargy which seemed to overcome her so readily. Young and strong, she had never felt a weariness like this before: a weariness just like Prue's.

She wanted to cry, wishing she had listened to Madge and gone back to London: wishing that Gaston was the kind of man that she had always thought him to be: wishing the clock could be turned back two weeks, and that she had never had that letter from Rose Beeton.

At least one thing was a relief. The sensation of someone touching her earlier must have been unreal, for Conan had not been in the house at the time: Conan had been in Oxford all day.

The comfort lasted for several minutes, long enough for her to take a sip or two of the milk which Tuesday had brought up a quarter of an hour before. It was not usual for the mistress's personal maid to bring round hot drinks, but perhaps, as Madge was ill, Tuesday had been told by Conan to look after his guest.

Then the bubble broke, and fear began to pluck at her again. She looked down at the tiny object catching the light of the lamp, reluctant to bend down and pick it up, because she didn't really want to know what it was.

But in the end she had to, and her fingers closed convulsively round it, her heart racing.

It was a cuff-link, and one which she had seen before. Made of solid gold, and very expensive, belonging to Conan Kilmartin.

Seven

Conan did not get back from Oxford until the following evening. He had sent a message, saying that his business was taking longer than he had thought, and because of this, and the storm, had not attempted the journey.

"I hope you haven't been bored."

Conan was drinking sherry in the sitting-room, ignoring his wife, but taking in every detail of Lalage's lilac gown, as if he were committing them to memory, because they were important to him.

"Not in the least."

Lalage gave her cousin a quick glance. In a few minutes, Crickett would be there to tell them that dinner was served, and there were things she wanted to ask Kilmartin. Seeing Prue's inattention, she plunged in.

"Conan, have you lost a cuff-link?"

"What a strange question." He considered the colour of his sherry against the light. "Yes, most excellent. I must tell Crickett to order more. No, not that I'm aware of. Why do you ask?"

She held herself very upright, determined to keep calm.

"Well, I found one, or rather, I thought I did."

He switched his attention from his glass to her, smiling.

"Stranger still. Either you did find one or you didn't . . . surely?"

"Yes, you must think it peculiar." She wouldn't look at

him. "But that is what happened. I found one last night, by my bed. It was one I had seen you wear, yet when I got up this morning, it wasn't on my dressing-table where I had put it."

The smile deepened.

"Oh dear. I do hope you're not getting delusions, like my poor wife."

Lalage thought him cruel to say such a thing in Prudence's presence, but it was obvious that her cousin hadn't heard Conan's words.

"So do I." She was short, pushing fear away. "I suppose someone must have taken it."

"I can't think why they should. In any event, I haven't lost one."

"It was solid gold, with a monogram."

He put his drink down, stretching out one arm.

"Like this?"

Lalage stared at the cuff-link on his wrist. She would liked to have thought it was a duplicate: to believe that Conan had two pairs exactly alike, but she knew she was clutching at straws. Finally she said:

"Yes, like that."

"What exciting dreams you have, and how glad I am that they are of me."

She blushed, but she wasn't done with him.

"There is another thing."

"Oh yes?"

"That portrait over there, by the window; the one in the oval frame. Who is she?"

"Arabella? She's the wife of one of my ancestors, but why does she interest you?"

"Because she is exactly like me. Oh, don't pretend you haven't noticed. She could be my twin."

"Arabella? Like you? My dear girl!"

"Are you saying that she isn't?"

"Most assuredly I am. She isn't remotely like you."

"Really!" Lalage got up abruptly. "You must be blind if you haven't seen the resemblance. Come and have a look."

He looked amused, although she couldn't imagine why.

"Very well, if it will satisfy you, but it won't make me change my opinion."

They walked over to the window, to the table and the port-rait hanging above it. Lalage felt disbelief creep over her, every nerve in her body jangling.

The face looking back at her was that of a woman of about fifty, with greyish hair and light blue eyes. Plump and opulent in velvet and diamonds, a small dog on her lap.

"I don't understand," she said finally. "It wasn't like this last night. The painting has been changed."

"No." Conan's eyes were half-closed as he watched her struggle with bewilderment. "It's always been there, as long as I can remember."

"But last night. . . ."

"Last night you found a cuff-link, or thought you did."

It was a blow under the heart, and she was still shaking when it was time to go into the dining-room. She didn't eat, and barely answered Kilmartin when he spoke. She was too busy thinking and worrying. Conan was right; she was getting like Prue. She made her excuses as soon as the meal was done, hurrying upstairs where she could be by herself, for she had to consider what to do.

She got to the first floor landing before she realised how dark it was. The gasoliers were out, only one oil-lamp on a table breaking the gloom. She couldn't understand why Crickett or Mrs. Parkington hadn't noticed what had happened, and come to rectify things. She groped her way along the wall, feeling as though she was being followed. When she heard the slight rustle behind her, she knew she had been right.

"Mrs. Parkington? Oh, I'm glad it's you. What is wrong with the lights?"

There was no answer, simply another faint sound as if a taffeta skirt were sweeping the polished boards. Lalage's throat felt constricted, her hands clenched at her sides. It wasn't the housekeeper, for now she could see a glimpse of crimson, and a slender white hand holding a lace-edged handkerchief.

"Oh no!"

She breathed the words, pressed up against the wall unable to move an inch. She wanted to call out for help, but all she could manage was a croak.

"Who . . . who are you? What do you want?"

"I won't let her stand in my way: I won't let you do so either."

The voice was low-pitched, not much more than a whisper, yet very penetrating. Lalage wasn't sure whether she recognised it or not. It had a curiously sexless quality, and now that her eyes were becoming more accustomed to the dimness, it seemed to her that the figure was tall for a woman.

"Who are you?"

No answer, but another warning.

"Go away, before it's too late. Don't interfere with things which are not your concern."

Lalage shut her eyes for a second, too frightened to move. When she opened them again, she was alone, and the terrifying thought that this was yet another illusion, like the cuff-link and the portrait, sent her rushing to her room.

To her surprise, Madge was there, peaky, but a welcome sight as Lalage slammed the door behind her.

"Gracious me!" Madge came forward quickly, taking Lalage's hands in hers. "Lovey, what is it? You're as cold as ice and you look as if you'd seen a ghost."

"I'm not sure that I haven't." Lalage gave a shaky laugh. "There was someone on the landing. I know you'll think I'm imagining it, but there really was. It spoke to me."

"It?"

Madge was settling her mistress into an armchair, getting out the smelling salts.

"No, no, I don't want those: they make me sneeze, you

know that. Yes, it said it wouldn't let me stand in its way. It also said it wouldn't let ' her ' stand in its way either. I think it meant Prue."

" Oh my dear, don't! " Madge put a comforting arm round Lalage's shoulders. " It's all these stupid tales you've been hearing. You thought it was that Mercedes, did you?"

" I suppose so. It was so dark, you see. I couldn't be sure."

" Dark? On the landing?"

" Yes, all the gasoliers are out. Go and see for yourself."

She waited, stiff with tension, until her maid returned, looking grave.

" All on. Bright as day out there. Now, don't worry any more. Just imagination, like you said yourself, and I'm not surprised in a place like this."

" But the cuff-link and the picture! "

Madge looked baffled as Lalage explained, words tumbling out of her.

" You see, it can't all be my fancy."

Madge said nothing, and Lalage felt her heart sink. Obviously, Madge didn't believe her, and now was not the time to tell her companion that she hadn't been at all sure that the person she had met outside was a woman. It could have been a man in disguise, but it was too tall for Crickett, and Conan had been in the dining-room.

Stiffly, Lalage got up, letting Madge help her to undress, as if she were a child. At that precise moment, she wished with all her heart that she was a child again, with all the care-free unawareness of the young. She certainly wasn't going to discuss the fact that if Kilmartin had no heir, Gaston Delorme's mother would inherit Amberstone, and that in the fullness of time, he himself would be its master. She wouldn't let herself think about the possibility that Gaston was responsible for Prue's condition; that he had somehow found a way of getting into the house to play pranks, first on her cousin, and now on her.

" I'm glad you're better," she said, when Madge pulled the

sheet over her. " But you'd better go and rest now. I'm quite all right again."

" Of course you are." Madge patted her hand, but she still looked worried. " Wish we'd never come to this dratted place. None of us will ever be the same, I know it."

*   *   *

It was on the following morning that Lalage heard Prudence begging Conan to let her see Denzil. There were tears in her voice which wrung at Lalage's heart.

" I promise I'll be good, Conan." Prue was humble. " Just for a moment, no more. I won't touch him, or upset him."

" No, you're in no fit state."

Lalage waited no more, quickly going into the garden so that she could avoid the rest of the conversation which was not for her ears.

She wanted to tax Kilmartin with his heartlessness, but to do that she would have to be alone with him, and she couldn't trust herself yet. Somehow, she had got to steel herself against him before she could fight Prue's battle for her.

By the sundial, she sat down, watching the peacocks preening themselves. Rose Beeton had thought them an affectation, but they weren't. They were part of Amberstone. They belonged there; they always had done.

She refused to let herself wonder how she knew that letting her thoughts slip back to Prue who wanted so desperately to see the baby she had tried to kill on the night of its birth. Reluctantly, Lalage had had to accept that fact. Too many people who had been there at the time had confirmed it.

The thoughts didn't stop at that, although she tried hard to hold them back. If Prue finally got her way, what would she see? An unusually silent baby, hidden somewhere in the house away from its mother, since his nursery was otherwise occupied, or would it be a monstrosity such as that born some fifty years before? Perhaps Conan was not so cruel, after all. If his son was in the north wing, perhaps he was right to stop his wife from seeing her child.

She didn't want to go into luncheon, but excuses would be hard to find. Her dismay increased when Conan announced that Prudence was in her room and wouldn't be joining them. Still, he couldn't do anything to her at one o'clock, in the glare of sunlight, and servants nearby.

"As there are only two of us, I have told Crickett to serve something cold in the garden-room." Conan had taken her arm. "We don't want to sit and stare at each other from opposite ends of the table, do we?"

Lalage would infinitely have preferred to do so, but the choice was not hers, and she was forced to take a chair at the table in the window.

She wondered what Kilmartin would say if she were to tell him that she had seen Mercedes the night before. She dared not risk it, lest he thought her demented too. Also, he might have seen her doubt about the apparition being his dead wife: Conan was uncomfortably perceptive.

She was nervous all through the meal, but he didn't seem to notice, keeping conversation to trivialities, at least until they had finished their coffee.

"I have to go over to Little Melton on business," he said finally. "I'm sorry to have to leave you again so soon, but I won't be long. Then we can . . ."

"It's quite all right, I understand."

She rose too, anxious to be gone, but he stood between her and the door.

"I'm sure you do." The smile was intimate. "You always understood."

"I . . . I must go."

"Of course. I'll let you know when I get back."

"I may be out."

"Then I'll leave a note for you."

It was no good. The fight was running out of her, like sawdust from a stuffed toy. He was closer, one hand cupping her chin.

" Please . . . Conan. . . ."

" Until later. Good-bye, sweetheart."

She could still feel his kiss minutes after he had left her, trying to pretend she hadn't been aroused. She was endeavouring to pull herself together, when she saw Mrs. Parkington in black straw bonnet, setting off down the drive.

It was the spur she needed. Conan had gone to Little Melton; Mrs. Parkington was out. It was another chance to look in the nursery; perhaps to find some clue as to where the real Denzil was, if, indeed, he existed at all.

She met no one on her way upstairs The servants had a short time to themselves before the preparation of the evening meal and other tasks had to be tackled. They would be in the kitchen, dozy in the heat, or gossiping over the tea-cups.

She told herself that she was optimistic to expect the nursery to be open, but it was. Turning the handle gently, she held her breath, jumping nervously when she heard the low crooning. Then she was inside, clinging to the door as she looked down at Prue, kneeling by the cot, cuddling something wrapped in a silk-fringed shawl.

" Oh, Lalage! "

Prudence was alight with joy. Her pallor didn't matter any more, nor the fact that there were dark rings under her eyes. The rapture on her face more than compensated for ill-health, and Lalage let her pent-up breath go in a shuddering sigh.

" So, he really is here. Oh, Prue darling, I'm so glad. So very glad."

She couldn't tell Prue what she herself had found in the cot. Prue wouldn't believe her, and in any event it didn't matter now. Denzil was back where he belonged, safe and sound.

" May I see him?" Lalage knelt beside her cousin. " I've wanted to, ever since I arrived. Dearest, may I?"

" Of course." The smile was full of happiness. " He's so beautiful. Look! "

The shawl was pulled aside as Prudence leaned forward.

Lalage could feel the world darkening, a sick faintness threatening to drown her. She saw the shining glass eyes and over-plump cheeks; the rosebud mouth, which was surely smiling now in a way it hadn't done before. Two rigid arms stuck up from its body, and Prue laughed.

" Oh look, do look! He wants you to hold him. Take him: feel how warm and soft he is."

Lalage couldn't move for a moment. She had to wait until the nausea passed and she was able to steady her voice.

" I won't, darling," she said finally, " I'm not used to babies, and I might drop him. But you're right; he is lovely."

" Yes, isn't he? I haven't seen him before, you know: they wouldn't let me." The blue eyes were mournful for a second: then they regained their wonder. " But to-day, Mrs. Parkington brought a tray to my room and said that she was going out. I ate everything, just as she said. I even drank all the milk, although I hate it. Then she told me that Conan was going over to Little Melton, and Crickett was visiting someone in the village. I knew then that my chance had come."

Somehow Lalage got to her feet. She had to get out of that room, for she couldn't bear Prue's false happiness a moment longer; couldn't stand the blank, but inimical stare of the doll either.

" I have to go, Prue. Don't . . . that is . . . don't stay too long. You should rest."

Outside, she leaned against the door, unable to walk. Poor, poor Prue. But the same question remained unanswered. The doll was still in the nursery, so where was Denzil, and what manner of child was he?

*　　　*　　　*

Lalage slept for two hours, waking at four-thirty. The first thing that she noticed as she sat up in bed was a white envelope which had been slipped under the door.

E

Her hands weren't steady as she opened it, yet she couldn't stop reading the note. She had known as soon as she had seen it that it would be from Conan, but why he wanted her to meet him in Devil's Dip, she had no idea. Then she understood. No one ever went to the Dip; everyone was too afraid of it. She and Kilmartin would be alone there.

At first she refused to consider the idea, dressing and tidying her hair. She was about to go downstairs, when Sabina arrived with a tray, giving her the same smirk that she always did, as if they shared a secret.

Lalage dismissed the girl with a cool word of thanks. She didn't like China tea very much, but she sipped it quickly, feeling refreshed as she put the cup down.

Afterwards, she couldn't remember exactly when it was that she decided to meet Conan. She looked in the mirror, realising that her gown wasn't the most attractive which she had with her, changing swiftly, and powdering her face anew. The perfume she used was heavy with musk, and normally she didn't like it, yet now it seemed entirely right. When she was certain that every hair was in place, she left the house by the side door.

There, she met Queenie Buncombe emptying a pail of dirty water. The child grinned at her, cheerful as ever.

" 'Ad to do the larder floor again," she said by way of explanation. " Cook said it weren't clean: more like a pig-sty she called it. Got a right ticking orf, I did, and no sit-down after the washin'-up were done."

Lalage looked down at the shrimp of a girl. Overworked, badly-clad, probably underfed, yet consistently buoyant in the face of every trial and tribulation. There was stout and real courage there, for Queenie was a survivor.

"Where is Devil's Dip?" she asked finally, opening her parasol. "I've heard so much about it, but I've never seen it."

As soon as the words were out of her mouth, she knew they weren't true. It was as if she were being given another glimpse behind the screen which separated past from present, and the route to the Dip was as well-known as the house and gardens. Then the flash was gone again: a door slammed shut. She waited for Buncombe to answer, fingers tighter about the handle of the parasol.

" 'Cor lumme, you're not goin' there, are you?" Queenie was aghast. " Shouldn't if I were you, Miss."

" No, of course I'm not going there." Lalage's lie tripped smoothly off her tongue. " I just wondered where it was, that's all."

" Just beyond the folly, down by Pope's Wood. 'Orrible place. Wouldn't catch me goin' there, not after what 'appened to the others."

" You really think that . . ."

" Somethin' got 'em." Queenie was vehement. " Went in, but never came out no more. You keep away, Miss."

" Oh, I shall. Thank you, Queenie."

Lalage hurried across the grounds and past the folly, finding a gate which led out to the woods. She saw the ground begin to slope downwards, still moving rapidly, for she didn't want to keep Conan waiting. Any thought that she was doing wrong had left her; since she had sat drinking her tea and re-reading his note, she had had nothing in her head but their meeting.

As she entered Devil's Dip, she was immediately aware of a strong sense of evil. There was no question but that she was in the right place, for it was exactly as it had been described to her. In the Dip, there was no hint of summer. It was a seasonless, timeless vacuum, girded by trees and crowned with a circle of dead water.

Conan wasn't there, and besides the sharp pang of disappointment, a wariness was wrapping itself about her. It was too quiet: nothing was moving. How long she stood there, she didn't know. Perhaps she might have remained frozen for ever, had she not heard the churning of water. Her head turned slowly, petrified as she stared at the pool. It was as still as ever, yet the noise was clamorous in her ears.

Whatever lay under the pond was rising to the surface.

She began to back away, screaming inside, stumbling on tree roots, rough briars and bushes catching at her carefully chosen dress. Then she heard the rustle behind her and cried out in relief:

"Oh thank God! Conan! Come quickly, quickly! There's something...."

Gaston Delorme stepped out of the shrubbery and eyed her coldly.

"Not Conan, I'm afraid, but will I do?"

She was horrified.

"Gaston! What are you doing here?"

"Exploring. Why shouldn't I be here? This is not private land."

"No, I know that, but..."

"But you expected Kilmartin, is that it?"

His smile was unamused.

"I'm sorry to disappoint you, but tell me: what were you saying just now?"

"What?" She was inattentive, still overwhelmed to find Gaston there, not having any idea of how she was going to explain her own presence, praying that Conan would hear voices and keep away. "I ... I ... don't know what you mean."

"Oh?" He let cool eyes travel slowly over her, and she knew he was seeing each rip and tear and the fear she couldn't hide. "It seemed to me that you were alarmed about something. Indeed, that is the exact word you used. Something."

"It's nothing." She tried to push a straying lock of hair back into position, but her fingers wouldn't obey her. "Really, it's nothing at all."

"Let me."

Gaston's touch was light and deft.

"There, that's better. Now you look as lovely as ever." The bantering tone was dropped abruptly. "Why were you meeting Kilmartin?"

" I wasn't."

" Come, you called out to him. Do you take me for a complete fool?"

" It isn't your affair."

" I hope it isn't your *affaire* either."

" I didn't mean that." She flushed. " You know I didn't. What I meant was that it was not your concern."

" I can make it so."

She heard the menace in his voice, and looked up apprehensively.

" Oh, yes." He nodded. " I can stop this very quickly. A note to your aunt, perhaps, to the effect that you have made an assignation with another woman's husband."

" You wouldn't!"

" I might, but there are other and more direct ways."

" I've no idea what you mean."

She couldn't look at him any longer: the shame was too great.

" Then let me make myself plain." His mouth was like iron. " Keep away from Kilmartin."

" Gaston." She was recovering from the terror of the water, and the shock of seeing Delorme. She was even able to face him again, but not easily. " What on earth has come over you? I've never heard you talk like this before. You've never cared about anything sufficiently to arouse such indignation."

" Indignation? Is that what you call it?" He hadn't relaxed a muscle. " It is quite a different feeling, I can assure you. Keep away from him; he is a dangerous man."

" Are you jealous?" She tried to make light of it. " I'm flattered."

" You have no cause to be," he returned uncompromisingly. " I'm not in the least jealous. Now I'm going to take you back to the house. Don't attempt anything like this again, or I shall take stronger measures to stop you making an exhibition of yourself."

" It's nothing to do with you, as I've said before." She tried to free herself from his hand. "Let me go, and mind your own business."

"I shall." He was grim. "Now, back to the house."

"Damn you! Let me go!"

"So that you can wait for Kilmartin, and roll in the grass with him like a village slut?"

Lalage hit Gaston across the mouth with her free hand. The comte didn't move, ignoring the trickle of blood running from the corner of his lip. At last, Lalage came to her senses, feeling as if someone had doused her with cold water.

"I'm sorry . . . oh, Gaston, I'm sorry. I didn't mean to do that. It was just that you made me so angry when you said. . . ."

"I haven't forgotten what I said." The hold had tightened. "See that you don't forget it either."

Lalage didn't know whether to laugh or cry at the absurdity of it all. The desire to meet Conan had quite gone, and now all that she wanted to do was to get away from Delorme's condemnation. It did look bad, of course, and he was right to berate her for wanting Prue's husband.

She wished she could have talked to Gaston about all that was troubling her so. There was so much that she wanted to confide in him, apart from Kilmartin's strange hold over her. The north wing, the doll, the cuff-links, and the portrait of a woman who looked so like herself, and which was no longer where she had seen it.

Yet she knew she couldn't explain to Gaston what Conan could do to her when he was near her; never explain that night, when Crickett had appeared as Conan was carrying her to his room; never tell him that a kind of madness overcame her now and then, when she craved for Kilmartin as a drunkard craved for spirits; never confess that she had no idea what had happened after she had fainted in Conan's arms.

Besides, there were other things to remember. She looked up again at the Frenchman's chilly face. One day, the comte might inherit Amberstone.

"Shall we go back?" she asked, when the silence couldn't go on any longer. "There's no need to break my arm. I'm not going to run away."

He let her go.

"Very well. Go straight back, and remember what I've said. Leave Kilmartin alone, or I shall kill him."

She felt as weak as a kitten when she reached the gardens and for a while she couldn't bring herself to go into the house. Instead, she sat by an ornamental pond, staring down at her reflection.

She wondered for a long time about Gaston's fury when he had found her waiting for Conan, yet he had said that he wasn't jealous. She realised that she resented his indifference. She wanted Gaston to care, but he hadn't, and so there must be another reason for his subdued violence and his final threat.

When she was in control again, still pondering on the anger in Gaston, she went to her room. She had reached the door when the truth struck her, and her mouth opened in consternation.

The only way Delorme would ever get Amberstone was if Conan had no heir. If Gaston knew that Denzil did not exist and that Prue was unlikely to conceive again in her poor state of health, did it mean that he thought Kilmartin might seek another wife, should anything happen to Prue? Prue was mentally unbalanced, and everyone knew it. Suicide was not impossible, and no one would be very surprised if she took her own life.

Lalage could feel her flesh prickling.

Had Gaston worked things out in such fine detail that he had assumed this a possibility, and that Conan, after a decent interval, might marry for the third time?

If Gaston had no sentimental reason for caring about her liaison with Kilmartin, there could be no other explanation. Not love or concern for her, but cold-blooded ambition and greed. She had thought Gaston a wealthy man, but perhaps his gambling had not been as successful as he had pretended.

If she had changed since she had arrived at Amberstone, Gaston had altered a good deal more, and she hardly recognised the man she thought she had known so well. Perhaps he wouldn't even wait for a suicide, which might not come.

Her hands were locked together so tightly that the knuckles were white, fear holding her rigid. It might be that the Comte de Lys was contemplating murder.

She swallowed hard as her stunned mind left Delorme for a second. Whatever Gaston was planning, it had not been he who had caused the sound of lapping water in the Dip. He had come out of the bushes behind her, so what was it that had been stirring beneath the weeds and water-lilies?

Eight

It was later that day when Lalage heard Mrs. Parkington's agitated whisper to Kilmartin.

" Only left him a moment, sir, I swear it, yet when I got back, he was gone. He just wasn't there. Crickett and I have looked, best we can, without making the others suspicious, but there's no sign of him."

Lalage could see Conan's face through the open door, hating herself for eavesdropping, but unable to resist the temptation. It was clear that the housekeeper was talking about Denzil, and Lalage needed to know about the boy. So, he did exist after all. She had been so sure of late that he had died at birth, that she had almost dismissed him. Now, she knew that he was alive, and the fearful question returned. If Conan's son lived, why was he hidden away?

She drew back quickly as Mrs. Parkington left the sitting-room, refusing to answer her own question. It was too horrible to think about. Instead, she braced herself to face Conan.

" Lalage."

He smiled, but she could see his thoughts were elsewhere.

" Conan, I must talk to you."

He gave a quiet laugh, all his attention on her now.

" I would rather make love to you."

" Be serious! Conan, I heard what Mrs. Parkington said."

The warmth drained from his eyes, his mouth hardening.

" Oh? You have taken to listening at key-holes?"

" The door was open."

" And the conversation private."

" I couldn't help overhearing, but in any event, I have been meaning to speak to you for some time about Denzil. I am not deaf, and I've heard rumours about him . . . that he may not be normal. I'm beginning to wonder if these stories are true. You will never let us see him; he never cries. And why do you torment Prue by putting that hateful doll in the nursery?"

" I'm not tormenting her. My dear girl, use your senses. The doll comforts her, and she's in no fit state to care for a baby, you can see that for yourself."

" I see other things for myself." She ignored the danger signals. " Such as the north wing."

She found herself being shaken so hard that her teeth rattled, gasping aloud as she landed on the floor with Conan standing over her. For a second she was terrified. His rage was not hot, but cold as ice. Ann's words came back to her yet again. Conan Kilmartin is dangerous.

" Damn you," he said finally. " Why did you come back? Why do you persist in interferring with things which are not your concern?"

" Come back? I don't know what you mean."

" Don't you?"

" No. I came here to see Prue."

The fury was gone, and he bent down to help her to her feet.

"Did you?"

His mouth was curving in a smile.

"Of course. Why else should I come?"

"To be with me again."

"Again? That's absurd. . . ."

She felt his mouth against her, unable to push him away.

"You stay because of me, don't you?"

"No! I . . ."

"Your Frenchman doesn't like it. I suspect he's in love with you, Liane, and who can blame him?"

"Lalage!"

"Of course; Lalage."

His hand was loosening the brooch of rubies and diamonds.

"Don't! Conan, stop it! One of the servants may come in; besides, I want my questions answered. What have you done with Denzil?"

He paused momentarily.

"I? Why should I do anything with him?"

"To prevent people seeing what he is really like." She knew the risk she was taking. Conan was a powerful man, and capable of fearful anger. "If you are innocent, why aren't you searching for him?"

"I have scarcely had time, have I?" The fingers began to move again, the brooch dropping to the carpet. "You were listening at the door, but when I've finished with you, I'll look for him, I promise you that."

"Please stop!"

"You don't really want me to."

"I do! I do! I hate what you do to me. I don't belong to myself when I'm with you. It's a dreadful feeling."

"You don't belong to yourself, but to me: you always have done."

The bodice of her dress was half-open, his hand cool against her flesh. She could feel the strong fingers moving gently; a touch so well remembered.

"Oh Conan . . . please . . . please. . . ."

She was in his arms, her resistance melting away under his kiss, but somehow she managed to try once more.

" Denzil."

" What about him?"

" If he is harmed . . . dead . . . Amberstone will go to Gaston's mother. You said so yourself. Could Gaston have taken the child?"

" He is capable of it, certainly, this beau of yours, but it makes no difference. Neither he nor his mother will get Amberstone. Your cousin may be out of her mind, but she can conceive again. I will have another son, no matter what has become of Denzil."

" Oh God! "

Lalage wrenched herself away, feeling like a slut with a dress half-undone, her hair disordered, loathing herself and feeling soiled. Under the humiliation there was an unbearable pain. Conan could make love to her, and talk of fathering another child with Prue whilst he was doing so. It was a battle between unhappiness and fury, and fury won.

" Don't touch me! " She jerked away from him, her voice ragged with anger. " Don't ever put your hands on me again. I hate you, damn you! Do you hear me? I hate you! "

She almost ran from the room, encountering the housekeeper in the hall. The woman's lip curled, but Lalage ignored her. At that moment she didn't care a jot what the servants thought of her; she was too concerned with the wounds she carried inside herself to bother with them or what they whispered about.

At last she managed to fasten the last button, forcing herself to be calm as she prepared to face Madge. Madge would notice at once that the brooch was missing, but she wouldn't know how it came to be lying on the carpet in the sitting-room.

Only she and Conan would ever know that.

*   *   *

After dinner that night, Lalage packed Madge off to bed, and then went out into the garden. At first, she had meant to walk for a while before retiring; to seek the solace of the summer darkness before she had to face another sleepless night. She wasn't aware of making a decision, but suddenly she found herself making for the folly. Although there was a moon, she knew that the tower would be gloomy, and she stopped at the gardener's hut, where she found candles and matches.

Nanny Peak was in her usual place, nodding as Lalage appeared.

"Hallo, dearie, come to have your fortune told again, eh?"

"No." Lalage wished she could see the woman's face, but it was as shrouded as before. "Have you heard that Master Denzil has disappeared?"

"Aye. I hear everything. What I don't learn from others, I read in the cards. Nothing misses me."

"Will he come back?"

"Don't know that yet. Maybe he will, maybe he won't."

"I suppose it doesn't matter." All at once, Lalage felt an overwhelming fatigue: weary and sick at heart. "If my cousin has another child, Mr. Kilmartin will still have his heir."

The silence became deadly, like a thick cloud hanging between the two of them. Then the wise woman stirred.

"Another child?"

The voice was a rasp on the nerve-ends.

"Yes." Lalage was too unhappy to feel the full extent of the anger in the air. "That's what he said. There is no reason why my cousin shouldn't have another."

"Never!" Nanny Peak spoke so quietly that Lalage scarcely heard her. "It's not in the cards. Never again; be sure of that. That girl will never carry another of Conan Kilmartin's children."

*　　　*　　　*

The next morning, Gaston Delorme rode over from Watermill to see Lalage. They went into the garden-room, where Worboys brought them coffee.

" Where is your cousin?"

Gaston was calmness itself, but under the surface his temper was almost blinding him, cursing Lalage for getting in the way of what was beyond her comprehension.

" In bed; she's not well. Cream?"

" You know perfectly well that I don't take cream. And what about Kilmartin?"

" He's out," she returned stiffly, ruffled by Gaston's tone. " I have no idea where, I'm afraid. No doubt one of the servants could tell you, if you're really interested."

" I'm not." He put his cup down abruptly. " What I am interested in is your return to London. I want you to go to-day."

Their eyes met. He looked so different that she hardly recognised him. How well he had concealed his real humour, and for so long.

" I cannot go to-day," she said finally. " Haven't you heard? Denzil is missing. Do you expect me to leave Prue at such a time? Of course I can't go home."

He didn't reply, and after a moment she said lightly:

" Do you think they'll find him?"

" Possibly." He leaned back in his chair, anger quenched for the time being. " Is a search being made?"

" Of course. That's what Conan is doing now. He's getting help from Priddy's Farm."

" Then I'm sure that if they are diligent, they will discover his whereabouts."

" If they don't, the police will have to be told."

She watched Delorme carefully, but his expression didn't change. If Gaston had been responsible for Denzil's removal, he was hiding his guilt very skilfully.

She dropped the subject, hoping to catch him out another way.

" You went riding with Prue the other day, I understand."

" Yes, my love. Why? Would you rather I had gone riding with you?"

" Not in the least."

She recognised her lie, her poise shaken. Why should she want to go riding with Gaston, when Conan . . . ? She pushed the question aside briskly.

" She said she nearly fell at the old quarry, yet you didn't notice. That's very strange. You are not usually so inattentive."

" No, I'm not. Prue had a lucky escape."

" This time." Lalage said it sadly, pouring herself more coffee because she wanted to get away from what she read in Gaston. " How is your mother?"

" My mother?" The tense moment was over. " Very well, as far as I know. Why do you ask?"

Lalage waited too long. She had been screwing up her courage to ask whether the comte knew Dominica would inherit Amberstone if Conan had no heir, but she had let too many seconds slip away, and now she was too nervous.

" No particular reason. I just wondered."

They didn't know what to say to one another. It made Lalage want to weep, for she and Gaston had been so close. There had never been the slightest barrier between them; now they were like strangers.

Then Delorme said quietly:

" Go home, Lalage. Go home to-day. Anything could happen to you if you stay here much longer."

*   *   *

Lalage had not slept properly since she had arrived at Foxcove, and that night was no exception.

Too many thoughts crowded her mind: too many people were not what they seemed. Denzil had gone, and Prue was inconsolable. They had had to give her an opiate to stop the hysteria, for the search of the surrounding countryside had given no clue as to the boy's whereabouts. And if he were discovered? Lalage cringed, and got out of bed quickly. It was no use lying there thinking of such things. She decided to get a book from the library: something very dull, which would encourage sleep to come.

On the first floor she paused. Prudence's room was close to the top of the stairs, and from it she could hear her cousin crying. The sedative hadn't worked after all. She took two steps towards the door, and then she heard Conan's angry voice, and stopped dead.

Kilmartin had lost one son, and now he wanted another. He had no thought for Prue, a sick and bewildered girl; he simply wanted her for one purpose only.

As she went slowly down the stairs, she felt like one dead. She should have been hating Conan for what he was doing to Prue, but all she could think of was her own longing to give him a child.

It was madness, and she recognised it. Gaston had been right: she should go home, before Amberstone and Kilmartin possessed her completely. She ought to leave, while there was still a tiny part of her own soul left. Yet as she picked a book at random, she knew she wouldn't go: not whilst there was a chance of Conan holding her in his arms again. All her disgust and anger had blown away like dust: if he had been with her at that moment, she would have begged him to love her.

On the return journey, she shut her ears to what was happening in Prue's room. If she wasn't careful, she would begin to hate her own cousin. When she got to the second floor landing, she heard a movement very close to her, and felt the chill of fear.

She couldn't see anything, yet she knew it hadn't been her imagination.

"Who . . . who is it?"

She wanted to scream and run up to the attics to Madge, but she was transfixed.

"Not you this time." The voice was filled with real venom.

" She will die first, then you. There will be no more sons for Conan Kilmartin."

When Lalage finally got back to her room, miraculously, Madge was there, relief flooding through her as she tried to keep her voice steady.

" I couldn't sleep. I went to get a book."

" So I see. We can't stay here any longer, you know that, don't you?"

" Yes, we'll go soon."

Lalage slipped into bed, Madge perching on the side.

" To-morrow."

" No, not to-morrow. We can't leave until Denzil is found."

" That may be too late."

" I don't know what you mean." Lalage tried a bluff. " Why should it be too late?"

Madge Commins shook her head.

" You know why. I've told you before, but you knew anyway. Dear God, what Lady Ann would say, I dare not think."

The almost rabid hunger for Conan had faded, and Lalage was in possession of herself once more. She wanted to lay her head on Madge's plump shoulder and tell her how frightened she was of what Gaston might be planning, and how helpless she felt whenever Conan touched her. But she couldn't. Pride, and something else, held her back.

" If you're concerned about Mr. Kilmartin, you have no cause. He's with Prue, not with me. I really did go down to get a book. See, here it is."

Madge glanced at the dusty volume lying on the bed, her eyes filling with tears.

" Oh, lovey, lovey," she whispered. " How I wish we'd never come here."

And that was the end of it. In the morning, Prue stayed in her room, Lalage accepting Conan's excuse that his wife was feeling unwell. He seemed very remote, talking to her as if she were someone he'd only just met, but she told herself stoutly that it was better that way, and was glad when he went off with the men to have another look for Denzil.

That afternoon, the fine weather broke, dark clouds gathering over the house and surrounding fields, thunder spots heralding a storm. When lightning split the skies open, Lalage went to the window of the music-room to watch the torrent. It was as if the gods were rising up, sending silver spears and rolls of heavy drums to warn mortals of their wrath.

When she saw Prue cross the lawn, her blue coat billowing madly in the wind, Lalage frowned. What could Prudence be doing out in such weather? Then she understood. Her cousin was going to Nanny Peak to see if she could help to find Denzil. She probably needed comfort too, after last night. Conan wouldn't have made any attempt to console his stricken wife. There had been other matters on his mind.

After some twenty minutes, Lalage left the room, tired of watching the raging elements. She paused on the second floor, looking upwards, wondering if Mrs. Parkington was in the nursery. The woman had seemed genuinely disturbed when she had told Kilmartin that her charge had gone, yet Lalage didn't trust her. Besides, Una Parkington was one of the very few people who had ever seen Denzil, and it was worth trying to talk to her again.

But when Lalage opened the door of the nursery, it wasn't the housekeeper she found, but her cousin, holding the doll and crooning over it as she had done before. It was a nasty jolt, but Lalage knew that she mustn't alarm Prudence.

" Hallo dearest. I'm glad you're feeling better. You got back very quickly."

" Back?" Vacant blue eyes met her own. " I haven't been anywhere."

" But I saw you. You were in the garden, going in the direction of the folly. I noticed your blue cloak."

" Not me." Prue's attention was back on her precious bundle. " I've been here with Denzil."

Reality had slipped away from Prue again. Her abject misery, when she had learned that the boy was missing, had quite gone. As far as she was concerned, her son was back, safe and sound in her arms.

" But I know I wasn't mistaken."

" Oh, that was Sabina. She had an errand to run; I lent her my cloak as it was raining so hard. Oh Lalage, isn't he beautiful?"

Lalage looked down at the painted china face, another twinge of fear running through her, but it wasn't until six o'clock that real panic began.

It was then that Crickett came hurrying in to announce that the gardener had found Sabina Tuesday's body, not a hundred yards from the folly.

" She was strangled, sir," he said to Kilmartin, out of breath through running to break the news. " Dead as a doornail when she was discovered. We've put her in one of the sheds. Will it have to be reported?"

Kilmartin was very calm.

" Yes, of course. Prue, I'm sorry. We'll have to get Worboys to help you until we can replace Tuesday. Yes, very well, Crickett. When this storm is over, we'll send to Little Melton. To-morrow, probably."

He could have been discussing the sale of vegetables, instead of the violent end of another human being, and Lalage was stunned. Not so much by Conan's indifference, but by the fact that she, Lalage, who believed it was Prue in the garden. If she had made such a mistake, had the person who killed Sabina made the same error?

She put her hand on Prue's shaking arm, but her thoughts were a long way off.

Had Sabina been meant to die, or should it have been Prue? The whisper on the upper landing the night before had said Prue: that odd, sexless voice, which could have belonged to a man or a woman.

Surely Conan wouldn't have wanted his wife to die: he

needed another son, and had said so, bluntly enough. And if not Kilmartin, who else would want Prue dead? The answer beat into Lalage's brain like hammer blows. If one of the servants at Amberstone were in Gaston Delorme's pay, it was most likely to have been the secretive Sabina. She would have enjoyed the intrigue and the money. She wouldn't have been reticent either, and would have told her paymaster what all the servants were gossiping about; Kilmartin, forcing his attentions on his sick wife.

That would mean Gaston had to be rid of Prudence, but, equally, he would want to silence his informant too, in case she betrayed him.

Whoever Gaston had strangled, if, indeed, it had been him, it wouldn't have mattered. Both Prudence Kilmartin and Sabina Tuesday had to die.

Nine

Lalage endured her fears until eleven o'clock that night. Dinner had passed off without incident, Mrs. Nuttall producing an excellent meal, and Crickett pouring claret as if nothing untoward had taken place.

Lalage, thinking of the lifeless body in the shed, was glad when she had been able to make her excuses and slip back to her room. Madge was irritable, nerves making her snappy.

" Oh, do go to bed," said Lalage finally. " I've told you that we shall be going home soon, but not yet."

" It'll be too late if you don't get away now. You should just hear what the staff were saying at supper to-night."

"I don't want to listen to servants' gossip," returned Lalage sharply. "Leave me, for goodness sake; I want to think."

"This place has changed you." Madge stopped in the doorway. "Always used to confide in me, you did. Now you want me out of the way, so that you can . . ."

"That's enough! Please go."

Lalage was ashamed of her ill-temper, but it was too late to call her maid back. To-morrow she'd make peace with Madge, for Madge had been right. She, Lalage, had changed, and the worry was whether that change would last for ever. Perhaps she would never again be the girl who had set out from London so short a time ago.

When she heard the snuffle of a horse, she went to the window. Still drenching down, but Conan in a thick cape was already riding off. Where did he go on so many nights? Another woman? The thought was dismissed quickly: she didn't want to think about Conan and another woman.

She couldn't settle to read, and her thoughts were poor company. It was then that a weary Belinda Isard tapped on her door.

Lalage was glad to see her: anyone would have been welcome at that moment, and besides, there was something she wanted to ask.

"Isard, you clean the sitting-room, don't you?"

Belinda was dropping with tiredness. Up at five-thirty that morning, she'd been on the go ever since. Up and down the stairs, never a moment's peace. All she wanted was to deliver her message and make for the attics, but she knew better than to be rude to one of master's guests.

"Yes, Miss."

"That portrait by the window: the one in the oval frame above a table. Do you know the one I mean?"

Isard stiffled a yawn, wondering why on earth Miss Lalage was bothering about pictures at that hour of the night.

"Not really."

"It's been changed. You must have noticed that."

Lalage was impatient, not seeing the girl's exhaustion in her own anxiety to get an answer.

"No, Miss, never looks at the pictures. I just dust 'em, that's all. Miss, I was told by Mrs. Parkington to tell you that the missus wants to see you in 'er room, if you can spare the time."

"Very well." Lalage sighed. How could anyone dust paintings every day of their life and not notice them? Then she saw the maid's pallor and eyelids which almost drooped. "That is all Isard."

There was no one in Prue's bedroom when Lalage got there: just a note lying on the bed. She knew she shouldn't be reading a letter not intended for her, but she couldn't help herself. Furthermore, the germ of dread was moving again. Prue had sent for her, but Prue wasn't there. Just the note.

She scanned the lines, the sense of fear deepening. It was from Gaston, but why should Gaston ask Prudence to meet him at the folly at this unearthly hour? The answer was painfully obvious, and Lalage turned and ran.

A stable-lad was startled from his sleep as she shouted to him, but with Lalage's assistance he soon got the mare saddled, and she was off, leaving the boy staring after her. Then he shrugged, too tired to worry about the vagaries of gentlefolk. Funny lot, anyway. He rolled himself over in the sweet-smelling straw and fell asleep again.

Lalage was soaked when she reached the folly, taking off her wrap and leaving it at the entrance. Almost at once she regretted it, for it was so cold inside. There was no candle this time, and only her small lamp provided a yellow patch in the darkness. Nanny Peak wasn't there, but neither were Prue and Gaston.

"Oh no!"

Lalage breathed the prayer silently. Perhaps she was too late. Prue might be lying anywhere inside the tower, dead, as Sabina Tuesday was dead. She began to move cautiously, keeping the light low, in fear that she might see Prue's body. She was so engrossed in her search that at first she was only aware of the sound of rain. When the tower door slammed to, she jumped, and it took a few moments to reassure herself that it was the wind which had been responsible, and not some ghostly hand.

She moved further into the folly, closer to the stone where Nanny's cards were normally spread out. Still no sign of Prue, or Gaston, but then she heard the first faint sound which made her turn quickly.

The noise grew louder as it came nearer to her: the same half-growl, half-snarl which she had heard once before, behind a locked door in the north wing. It ought to have been an animal, but it wasn't. Lalage backed away, the light in her hand dancing as she shook like one with the ague.

So this was where Conan had brought his freak of an off-spring: this was why he rode out so often at night. There must be someone else who kept an eye on the creature when Conan wasn't there; probably another servant whom Lalage had never seen. A man, or woman, paid well to do a dreadful job when Denzil had been moved from the north wing to the folly.

Now the sounds were closer than ever, and Lalage's back was against the wall. There was nowhere else she could retreat to: no way now of knowing in which direction the door lay, for she had lost her bearings as she had done once before.

Slowly, like one in a trance, she raised the light, screwing up every last ounce of courage to face what was shut up in the tower with her. Just for a second the thought flashed through her mind that Denzil was only six months old. If he could make sounds like this now, what would he be like in a year's time?

The last thing she expected to see was a crimson gown, falling in ruffles to a small train. As Lalage raised the lamp higher still, she could see milk-white hands, wearing expensive rings, and then a long, slender neck, and finally a perfect, oval face, framed with black hair.

" Mercedes"

She recognised the woman at once, for she had seen enough portraits of her on the walls at Amberstone. She couldn't believe what her eyes were telling her, and the awful noise was still going on.

" You're dead!" Lalage's voice was barely audible. " You can't be here; you died in Devil's Dip. You're dead! You're dead!"

The soft laugh and the whisper were the same as those she had heard on the landing.

" Not I, my dear, but you will be soon. You've stood between Conan and me for so long. Whilst you are here, he'll never love me as I love him."

Lalage saw the fine cord wound round the woman's hands, but she couldn't move. The lamp was taken from her helpless fingers, and she could smell perfume, heavy and intoxicating. Then she felt the cord slipped round her neck. She didn't know why she stood still: part of her brain was crying out to her to fight, but her body wouldn't obey. She could do nothing but wait, feeling the constriction tightening, the noise deafening her as she waited to die.

She hardly heard the pistol shot. All she knew was that the pressure on her throat was gone, and that the woman's eyes were wide open with surprise. Then the ribbon of blood running down the chin, and finally the slight thud as she collapsed at Lalage's feet.

Over her body, Kilmartin and Lalage looked at each other, Conan remarkably unmoved as he slipped the gun inside his coat. She was safe from strangulation, but not free from whatever it was that was behind Conan, and she whimpered.

" Conan . . . Conan . . . that noise. It's Denzil, isn't it? You brought him here from the house, didn't you? Oh God, I was right: there is something wrong with him, but I don't want to see him. Oh, please, please, don't make me look at him, I couldn't bear it!"

Kilmartin held out his hand, as if to draw her nearer to

whatever was at his back. Lalage screamed, until the cries deafened her, shrieks whirling round her head as blackness engulfed her and carried her away from harsh reality.

*   *   *

When Lalage regained consciousness, she was in the sitting-room at Amberstone. The grey stone walls of the folly, the smell of dampness and death, and the ghastly sounds had all vanished. Madge was there, patting her hand, casting an occasional worried glance at Prudence.

Lalage moved her head until she could see Gaston by the window, and Conan, sitting on a chesterfield, a large black dog at his side. The animal had bright, intelligent eyes, its head cocked, as if waiting to see which of them would break the silence. Crickett and Mrs. Parkington were there too, the latter stiff as a ramrod on her upright chair, no vestige of expression on her face.

In the end, it was Lalage who spoke. She sat up, ashamed that her voice quavered, determined not to let the swaying room make her faint again. Conan would think her a weakling: Mercedes would not have broken down in such circumstances.

"I don't understand," she said. "Gaston? Conan? what happened?" She shut her eyes for a second, re-living the appalling moment in the tower. "I saw Mercedes, or, at least, I think I did, and I heard. . . ."

Delorme moved forward, resting a hand on her shoulder.

"Don't be afraid, Lally," he said quietly. "There's no need for it now. As to what happened, I suggest you ask Kilmartin, for all that has taken place was brought about by him, and his wife, Mercedes."

Lalage turned back to Conan. He was very still, like a man already dead.

"Conan?"

Finally he raised his shoulders.

" Very well, I suppose it doesn't matter any more. It's over anyway."

He took a thin cigar from his case, lighting it carefully before he spoke again.

" It began because Mercedes couldn't have children, and I needed an heir. That meant more to me than anything else in the world, and she knew it. She worked out a plan whereby I could have a son, and she could remain my wife. I think she was afraid that she would lose me, and so she was prepared to make sacrifices."

As he continued, Lalage shrank back against the cushions supporting her. Reduced to essentials, Conan's story was one of obsession and passion. He was obsessed with the desire for an heir. Mercedes loved him with a passion strong enough to contrive the death of others to keep him.

Their first move had been to kill Nanny Peak, and then to stage Mercedes' drowning in Devil's Dip. Shortly after Mercedes ' died ', Nanny reappeared. Mercedes, who had spent much time with the old woman in the past, had not only taken her life and identity, but her clothes, her simples, herbs and drugs, her Tarot cards, and finally her hut, where Conan visited her several nights each week.

In order to keep prying villagers and others away, the old legend of the pool was given new flesh and substance. Two of the girls from the village, who had been bold enough to enter the dell, had seen Mercedes without her disguise, and had died for their pains. Their end had helped to keep the tale alive.

The next step was for Conan to ' marry ' again; a young woman who could bear him a child, and Ephraim Oldacre's dire financial straits provided the answer to this problem. Since Mercedes had no intention of remaining in the hovel in Pope's Wood for ever, the systematic drugging of Prudence had begun almost at once. Mercedes, and her personal maid, Sabina Tuesday, had learned a lot about Nanny's potions, not all of them harmless. With the help of Crickett and Mrs.

Parkington, it hadn't been difficult to feed the innocent and inexperienced Prue with insidious doses of hallucinatory and other drugs, which had kept her hovering on the borders of madness, or in a state where she couldn't remember her actions or what she had said. Eventually, a faked suicide would end her life.

"But how could Mercedes have hoped to come back from the dead without creating suspicion?" Lalage stirred, chilled to the bone. "Everyone knew that she had died. How could she explain?"

Kilmartin eyed her thoughtfully. She was still the most beautiful woman he had ever seen. The slight loss of weight, and her pallor, gave her a new fragility which made her even more vulnerable and desirable. He had loved Mercedes, in a way. She had been exciting in bed; stimulating as a companion; a good hostess to his friends and neighbours. But she had never touched his heart as this girl had always done. He looked back at the tip of his cigar.

"That wouldn't have been so hard," he said at last. "She would have come back to Foxgrove when Denzil was a year old, and we were sure that he was strong and healthy. She would claim to have lost her memory and wandered off." There was a flicker of humour in him. "Mercedes favoured a story that she had been found by gipsies, and had travelled with them until she remembered who she was. I always thought that a trifle fanciful. However, it isn't important now."

"I can't believe it." Lalage had seen and understood Conan's look, turning her head away from his need for her. "I can't accept that people could be so wicked. I understand how much you wanted a son, but to kill innocent people . . ." She looked back at Conan. "There are still many other things to explain. Who was it who struck me in the tower that night?"

"Mercedes. I was there too, but I wasn't in time to stop her."

"And the feeling that I had that someone was watching me?"

"Someone was; Sabina. She was very soft-footed, and Mercedes had told her to keep an eye on you, and to report to her all that you said and did. It was Sabina who told Mercedes you intended to visit the folly."

Prue was crying softly, and Madge shook her head, but Crickett and the housekeeper were totally unmoved. There was neither fear nor remorse in them because of what they had done. Death had meant nothing to them.

"I'm sure Mr. Kilmartin hasn't finished." The comte was short. "Please go on, sir."

"Very well, although from our brief discussion just now, it seems that you, at least have guessed the rest of it."

"Very probably, but confirmation will do no harm."

Lalage managed to get up at last, going to Prue.

"Yes, do go on, for if Gaston has understood everything, I certainly haven't. What about Denzil? Why did you hide him? And why was Prue never allowed to see him?"

"Because Mercedes didn't want the child to belong to Prudence in any way. He was to be our child; Mercedes' and mine. That is why we didn't let Prue near him."

There was a shadow in Conan's eyes which Lalage didn't like, and for the first time since he had started his confession, she was not sure that he was telling the truth.

"We gave her a doll," he went on, "and she seemed happy enough with that."

"You are a monster!" Lalage was almost breathless with anger, her fear forgotten for a moment. "How could you do anything as heartless as that?"

"I didn't find it difficult."

"Conan."

It was Prue, holding Lalage's arm tightly to give herself courage, her face drawn with pain.

"Yes?"

Kilmartin looked at her as if he had never seen her before.

"I can't remember things properly, and now I know why, but I do seem to recall something horrible that you said to me. I could never be quite certain, but it was about the night Denzil was born. Did you say that I had tried to . . . ?"

"Kill him?" He was sardonic. "Yes, I did, and fortunately you believed me. So did the servants, and that is why no one was particularly surprised that we wouldn't let you care for him. Now and then, Mrs. Parkington would let slip the fact that you refused to see your son. The staff lapped that lie up as readily as the first, and it soon spread to the village. It is all too simple to fool the gullible, if one knows how."

"But I didn't, did I?" Prue was in agony. "I didn't try to harm my own baby, surely?"

"No, if it's any consolation to you, you never saw him. The servants didn't hear or see anything either, come to that. They simply believed Crickett and Mrs. Parkington when they described your attempts to strangle the child as you screamed like a madwoman."

"Oh, thank God!"

"I shouldn't be too ready with your gratitude to the Almighty. He's gone; Denzil, I mean. You won't see him again."

Once more Lalage saw a flash in Conan's eyes which she couldn't fathom. Not regret or sorrow, but relief. Relief that his precious heir had gone? It didn't make sense, unless . . . She dared not let herself dwell on that subject, nor could she bear Prue's suffering, changing the subject quickly.

"What had Fanny Thurston done? Why was she murdered?"

"She was unfortunate, that's all. She saw Mercedes and me together in the folly. We couldn't let her live after that."

"Human life doesn't mean much to you, Conan, does it?" Lalage was enduring her own tortures. "No one mattered to you, did they?"

"No, save for one person."

Their eyes met once more, and Lalage shivered.

"You told me that Gaston would inherit, through his mother, if you had no heir. Was that true?"

"You are too credulous by half." The scorn was back. "I simply wanted your doubts falling elsewhere for a time. Neither he nor his mother have any connection with my family."

"Thank God for it," said Gaston shortly.

He would have said more, but Lalage was not yet finished.

"That day you sent me a note, asking me to meet you at Devil's Dip, I heard movements under the water." It was Lalage's turn to cling to Prue, needing human warmth to stop the blood running cold in her veins. "There really is a thing beneath the surface, isn't there?"

Conan was derisive.

"Beautiful, but stupid."

The fear went, and healthy anger took its place.

"Stupid? You mean that was a trick too?"

"Of course, what else could it have been? On the far side of the Dip, screened by bushes, there is another pool. All Mercedes had to do, when anyone came into the clearing, was to agitate the water. That soon drove them off: not that many came."

Kilmartin lay back in his chair, his voice regretful.

"I'm sure that it will give you utmost satisfaction to hear that the plan didn't work out as I had expected it to do. I hadn't reckoned on Mercedes' jealousy of you. She was afraid of you, and that is why she told you those tales when she was pretending to be Nanny Peak. She wanted to frighten you away. She suggested that you be given drugs, as Prue had been, so that you were no longer certain of what you were doing. We knew exactly how to create illusions, you see." The faintest smile touched his lips. "Whilst Tuesday was doctoring your tea and coffee on Mercedes' instructions, I had had a better idea. At first, I thought of sending you packing, but then I realised that wouldn't work. You were suspicious and spirited, and I didn't think you would simply walk away. I decided to make you love me."

"What!"

"Oh, yes." The grey eyes were mocking. "Mercedes set out to make you believe you were as crazy as your cousin: I set out to get you into my bed." His mouth twisted. "I thought I was succeeding admirably, surprised that you gave in so easily. It was only a day or two ago that I learned Sabina and my wife had quarrelled. Mercedes had given the girl a sound beating, and Sabrina was a spiteful bitch. She knew just how to hit back. She changed the drugs you were being given. She started giving you aphrodisiacs almost as soon as you arrived."

He glanced at Lalage's stunned face.

"Do you know what they are?"

"Of course." She coloured uncomfortably, ignoring Gaston's muttered oath. "But I don't think I want to hear . . ."

"I'm sure you don't, but you will nevertheless. The comte has decreed that this is the time for truth, and truth he shall have. You responded to me so readily that I was surprised. I had expected you to repel me, but instead you would have slept with me, wouldn't you? But perhaps it wasn't all Sabina's draught."

"Damn you!" De Lys was violent. "Watch what you are saying."

"You don't like the thought? You should have remembered that truth is a double-edged weapon."

It cost Lalage a supreme effort, but she had to know, and she forced herself to ask.

"So Mercedes, with Sabina's help, tried to make me think I was mad, and you tried to seduce me so that if I did discover anything I wouldn't give you away, but there is one thing I have to know. Conan, that night when I fainted: do you remember?"

"Very clearly."

He switched his attention from Gaston's fury to her anxiety.

"I don't know what happened after that. Are you going to tell me, or will you leave me wondering for the rest if my life?"

"Yes, that would be in character, wouldn't it, but for once I'll be generous. My dear comte, do sit down." His tone hardened. "You asked me to explain, and I'm doing so. I'm sorry if the result offends you. Nothing happened, Lalage. I took you back to your room, and there I left you. It was a remarkable piece of self-control on my part, don't you think? After all, you were half in love with me, weren't you? It would have been so easy to have waited until you had recovered, and then to have . . ."

"Be careful." De Lys was still rigid, his anger increasing. "My patience is not boundless."

"I'm sure it isn't." Conan was unmoved. "And now, sir, may I hear from you? Why did you start to meddle in the first place, and how did you guess the truth, or, at least, most of it?"

Gaston sat down, the heat leaving his voice.

"I hadn't the least intention of meddling." He shrugged. "It was sheer coincidence that I went to stay with the Lauries at the same time as Lalage came here. You must remember that I have known her for years: we grew up together, although we haven't seen much of one another in the recent past.

"I could see at once that she had changed: she was a completely different person, and obviously very unhappy. She was also secretive which is not like her at all. In the old days, she would have confided in me at once. As it was, she tried to avoid me. I assumed, I'm afraid, that she was involved with you, and not only emotionally. I sensed there was more. I'm sorry, Lalage."

Lalage blushed. If only Gaston had known of what she

suspected him to be guilty. He didn't wait for her to speak, but went on.

"I asked myself what you and she could possibly be doing, and for some reason I connected it with your son; the child only you and the housekeeper had ever seen. You wanted an heir so much, yet when you got one, you hid him away. There could have been good reasons, as you tried to pretend, but I thought otherwise. It was obvious that, in the end, he would have to be seen. He couldn't remain invisible for ever. Therefore, I took it that there was a point in time for which you were waiting."

Kilmartin was dry.

"Such acumen. I didn't think you capable of it."

"No, most of my acquaintances would agree with you." Gaston smiled thinly. "My reputation is not one which encourages people to believe me intelligent."

"It is clear that they, and I, are wrong. Do go on: I am most interested."

Gaston gave Lalage a straight look.

"This will hurt, Lally, but as Mr. Kilmartin has pointed out, truth often does. A time-limit? A time when the child could be produced. What were the pair of you waiting for?"

Lalage swallowed hard.

"W . . . what did you decide?"

"That you were waiting for your cousin to die."

"Oh, Gaston!"

"Yes, I know, I know. I'm sorry; truly sorry. I saw the state Prue was in. I wondered if someone was driving her to her limits."

"And you were right." Kilmartin smiled. "But you were wrong about the identity of my accomplice. What was your next move?"

Lalage turned away from Gaston's cold face, because she couldn't bear to look at him any more. Instead, she glanced at Conan. He was not afraid, even though he faced dire consequences. He was cool and collected; even amused.

"I'm not sure I would have made another move, in the circumstances. I loved Lally, and I think I would probably have gone away and left her with you, especially as she seemed to favour this."

"Perhaps she did. Yet you didn't go. Why not?"

"I had a piece of unexpected luck. I'd been questioning people, including some of your servants, the honest ones." Gaston laughed shortly. "My instinct told me who they were. I learnt all about Devil's Dip, the north wing, and Nanny Peak. I also spoke to a village woman about Nanny. She had been treated by her for years: a skin complaint, for which an ointment was given. Nanny had told the woman never to use a particular herb. Then, some two years ago, the ointment was changed: it contained the very herb she had been warned not to use. She recognised its smell. She continued to visit the folly because she was afraid to offend, but she never used the ointment again."

Gaston paused, and Kilmartin watched him. Under his bland exterior, Conan was genuinely surprised. He hadn't thought the Frenchman particularly shrewd, but he'd been wrong. The comte was not only clever, but persistent. Delorme went on.

"Obviously, the real wise woman would never have made such a mistake, and so after that I worked from the premise that another had taken her place. Naturally, I didn't think of your wife, but of someone hired to serve your ends."

"Even more astute. I congratulate you. And then?"

"After that, I considered again what the motive was for all this. Three young girls had died: Sabina Tuesday was strangled. When people disappear or are killed, there has to be a reason. Often, it is money, but I knew it wasn't so in this case. It had to be something else.

"As Lally's reputation became more besmirched, I grew so furious that I could scarcely be civil to her. I think I almost hated her for a while. I believed her to be a whore and an adventuress, and yet something in me could not accept that

F

she knew the whole truth of what she had got herself into.

"I began to follow her, and you too, Kilmartin. I saw you go to that hut in Pope's Wood on several occasions at night. I believed you were meeting Lalage there, and I wanted to kill you both, yet I could not go to the hut to confirm my suspicions. I couldn't have borne to see you and Lally together. But earlier to-day I made myself go, and this time I saw you with the woman in the portrait. Your wife; Mercedes."

He could see the tears on Lalage's cheeks, yet he couldn't comfort her just then; not in front of Kilmartin.

"She was alive," he said after a moment. "Her death had been a mere pretence. Then I knew I was right about Prue's condition: someone had been trying to make the world think her mad. Not Lally, but your wife. You would have killed her eventually, wouldn't you?"

"Of course."

Prue shuddered, and Gaston went on again.

"I realised too that such a woman would have a plausible story for returning to her home in the fullness of time, after Prue was dead, and then you, she and the child would be together. Otherwise, there would have been no point in your plan. Denzil would have to be seen in order, one day, to inherit."

Kilmartin was cautious.

"Yes, that was the idea."

De Lys took time before he spoke, as if he were pondering on Kilmartin's tone.

"To-night I came to Amberstone to force Lalage to tell me exactly what part she was playing in all this. I still believed her guilty of something: of aiding and abetting you and your wife, because she was in love with you. I had to know the extent of her involvement before I did anything. A maid said she was in Prue's room, but she wasn't there. I went to look for myself, and it was then that I found the note purporting to come from me to Prue. I was almost too late: indeed, I was too late. Lalage would have died, but for you."

Conan gave a faint sigh.

" Yes, I see. You have been most industrious, and correct in most of your guesses. Mercedes was growing tired of the role she had chosen for herself. She nagged me constantly for not hastening Prudence's end. I told her I could do nothing whilst Lalage was here. We often quarrelled, especially of late. Once, she clawed my face, and I'm afraid I let Prue take the blame for that. I went to her that night: in the darkness, she didn't see the scratches, but when Lalage noticed them the next morning, she assumed they were Prue's doing. Then Mercedes found out I proposed to father another child."

Kilmartin's face had grown as cold as stone.

" In the end, Mercedes had her revenge. She took Denzil. I expect Tuesday helped her; someone in the house would have had to do so. Probably that is why Sabina had to die; to keep her quiet. Either that, or Mercedes discovered that she was giving Lalage the wrong drugs. Mercedes couldn't bear me to look at another woman. She even resented Prue, although she knew I didn't care a fig for her."

Prue flinched, and Lalage said hotly:

" She must have been insane, as well as wicked."

" Probably we were both a little mad to try what we did, but I needed a son, and Mercedes needed me, until she thought I was being unfaithful to her." His eyelids closed, so that no one could read his thoughts. " Now we shall never know what happened to Denzil."

For a split second, Lalage thought she could see a glimmer of a smile on his lips; the merest hint of thankfulness in his voice.

Then Delorme said smoothly:

" Oh, but you shall know, for it wasn't your wife who took him, but I. I removed him, with a little help from one of your servants, who shall remain nameless, and I can assure you that he is quite safe. You really should keep that side door locked, you know. Anyone can come and go at will. Now that his milk is not tampered with, your son is thriving and yelling like any six-month-old infant should do."

Conan opened his eyes, frozen, as if in a deep coma.

" What! "

" I said I took him." Delorme considered the signet ring on his finger reflectively. " You need have no further worries. He is safe."

Lalage watched Conan closely, feeling cold again. Not relief, nor delight, that his son was safe, but stark, unmistakeable shock. Then she turned to Gaston, and the dread increased. A thread was passing between the two men: a silent communication, which she didn't understand; as if they were sharing a terrible secret.

" Conan." She could hardly get the words out, but they had to be said. " Those rumours about the north wing. I went up there one day; there were sounds. It was the same noise that I heard in the folly to-night. What was it?"

As one blind, Kilmartin turned his head in her direction, taking a whole minute to control himself.

" Oh that. It was only Jonus." He stretched out a hand to pat the huge dog's head. " He always grows savage when he's shut up for too long. We did that deliberately to keep the servants away from that part of the house. In the tower to-night, I chained him up again, and he didn't like it. Mercedes wanted to kill him, but I wouldn't let her."

Lalage looked down at Jonus. As she watched, he stretched himself out on the hearthrug, nearly the size of a young calf, thumping his tail in satisfaction. He seemed docile and entirely contented, but then he wasn't chained up at that moment.

" So the rumour that your family is cursed, isn't true? That once every fifty years or so. . . ."

" Dear God!" Kilmartin had managed to subdue whatever deep emotion had had him in its grip. " How gullible can a woman be?"

" It was made up, to scare people, and to keep them away from Denzil?"

" Of course," he returned lightly. " It was most effective."

Lalage wanted to believe him. More than anything else in the world she wanted to believe him, but she couldn't, yet to pursue the matter would be to give her cousin more pain. However, she herself now had to hurt Prue, and she kissed her gently, as if asking for forgiveness in advance.

"You wanted Prue to have another child. Why, if you had Denzil?"

The dark brows rose.

"Scarcely a delicate subject for a well-brought up young woman, but since you ask, yes, I did want another son. If Denzil had not lived beyond infancy, it would have been necessary to have another before Prue died."

"Oh no!"

"Don't Prue. Oh, my love don't!"

Lalage held her cousin close, feeling the slight frame shake in her arms.

"It's all right, sweet, you'll soon have your baby back, won't she, Gaston?"

The question was sharp, as if she were challenging Delorme, but he merely nodded.

"Very soon. Don't grieve, *madame*, he has come to no harm."

Again there was the odd look between the two men, but Lalage ignored it this time. Its implications were too horrifying to contemplate, and she turned to other questions.

Kilmartin said that Tuesday had put his cuff-link by Lalage's bed, and later removed it: it was to make her doubt her own senses, yet also to tie her closer to him. Conan did not say whether he had really been in Oxford that day or not, and Lalage couldn't bring herself to ask. It was better to assume that her sleep had been a disturbed one, due to a doctored drink: the feel of someone's hands on her all part of the stupor.

Kilmartin hadn't know about the letter on the bed, which Crickett had forged, copying Gaston's handwriting from a note he had written to Prue, thanking her for her hospitality.

Mercedes had not told him of her instructions to Mrs. Park-ington to make sure that Lalage saw it. Conan had simply gone to the folly that night to see Mercedes, taking Jonus with him.

Mrs. Parkington's slowness in opening the nursery door when Prue knocked on it, and her apparent sojurns there for hours on end were no longer a mystery. There was another exit from the nursery, which led up a narrow flight of steps to the attics in the north wing. There, the housekeeper had a small sitting-room, with a fire on which she could boil a kettle, and a few sticks of furniture.

Every last detail of Conan's inhuman and uncaring under-mining of Prue's sanity was uncovered, even the remark he had made to his housekeeper about having his wife put away: a comment she was meant to hear. Each bite of Mercedes' cruelty to Prue, when the girl had visited her, believing her to be the wise woman, was laid bare. Nothing was spared. Kilmartin was as brutal to Prudence as he had always been.

Mercedes had come into the house now and then, allowing herself to be seen by Prue, partly to terrorize her and partly to foster the story of the ghost. The doll had been provided, not to console Prudence, but to underline her growing madness.

Finally, Gaston said:

" Well, there seems little else to explain. Sir, I am taking your confederates to Watermill with me. When I get there, I shall send for help. Do I make myself clear?"

Conan smiled faintly.

" Perfectly, and I am grateful."

" I am not doing it for you."

" I know that."

The comte signalled the two servants to the door, taking Prue's arm.

As Lalage passed Kilmartin she paused and they looked at each other, oblivious to the others. Then Conan raised her hand to his lips.

" Good-bye, Liane," he said softly, " until the next time."

She couldn't answer him, and there was a lump in her throat as she followed Delorme out into the torrential rain. It was as though she were leaving a precious and vital part of herself behind.

Gaston wouldn't let them wait in the house whilst the odd-job boy rushed off to the stables with orders that a carriage be made ready. Madge protested vigorously, but the comte paid her no heed, herding them along the drive, as if he wanted to get them away as soon as he could.

When she heard the shot, Prudence moaned and covered her face, but Crickett and the housekeeper hardly paused in their tracks. Any humanity or feeling they had had in them had drained away long ago.

Lalage began to run back, only to feel hands like iron on her shoulders, restraining her.

" Gaston! Let me go! Let me go! Don't you understand what he's done?"

" Of course." The comte was icily calm, pelting rain darkening his blond hair. " Would you have preferred to see him hang?"

He left her then to speak to the coachman, and Lalage was grateful to be alone with her grief, if only for a moment. She stood there, unaware of what was going on behind her, or the roughness of the wind, thinking only of Conan.

Gaston had said there was no more to be explained, but he had been wrong. She tried to accept the explanations given a short time before: tried to pretend there had been no more to it than well-worked out scheme by two ruthless people and their helpers, but she couldn't fight her doubts any longer.

She hadn't been drugged on the afternoon she had arrived at Foxcove. She had been certain from that very moment that she had seen the house before; had lived there, and loved it well. She even knew where the small, unobtrusive side door had been, although no one had shewn it to her: the music-room was a well-loved place: the peacocks were old friends.

When Conan had ridden up to her that afternoon, which

seemed a life-time ago, she had known beyond doubt that it hadn't been their first meeting.

It was an impossible belief, but she couldn't rid herself of it. Tuesday might have put things in her milk and coffee, but she couldn't have given her that unshakeable conviction that she belonged both to Amberstone and to Conan Kilmartin.

He had told the others that he had made love to her to keep her silent, but she knew that that was a lie. What was in his eyes when he said good-bye was the real truth.

She tensed as another thought struck her. She couldn't imagine why it hadn't occurred to her before, or why Gaston hadn't raised the question. Although Kilmartin had shewn her nothing but contempt for the last half hour, when he had had to make a deadly decision, he had done so without hesitation. He had saved her life, at the expense of Mercedes', and Gaston had not even asked why.

She turned away, walking over to the housekeeper. The woman's dress was sodden, clinging to her body, her face totally blank.

" That portrait which Mr. Kilmartin put away. Who was she?"

At first, Lalage thought Mrs. Parkington wouldn't reply, but finally she said grudgingly:

" Wife of one of his forebears."

" Her name?"

" Liane."

Lalage felt as if someone had walked over her grave.

" And her husband? What was the name of Liane's husband?"

At last the stony glare moved to Lalage, and for the first time there was some expression to be seen. Hatred; naked and undisguised.

" Conan. Same as the master."

The housekeeper walked off, so that she didn't have to answer any more questions standing by Crickett as the carriage rumbled towards them.

Lalage remained motionless until Delorme called to her to hurry, as he helped Prue and Madge into the coach. It was as if she were coming out of a coma as she looked back at Amberstone for the last time, wiping moisture from her eyes. It could have been rain, but she didn't think so.

"Good-bye, Conan," she whispered finally, glad that Gaston was too far away to hear, for he wouldn't have understood. She didn't really understand it herself ." Good-bye, my love, until the next time."

* * *

For the next seven months, Lalage lived in an unending social whirl. She attended every dinner-party, concert, ball, and soirée to which she was invited, entertaining at her own home in lavish and frenetic style. She had to pack her life full of ordinary people, and laughter, and frivolity, so that the remembrance of Conan could be kept at bay, and the thought that she had lost Gaston, smothered beneath the chatter and gossip of her friends.

When she went to see Ann each morning, she was very careful to be the light-hearted girl her aunt was used to. She thought she had fooled the old lady, until one morning, when her smile was more artificial than usual, Ann said gently:

"Dear, brave, Lalage, I'm proud of you. Whatever it is, my love, it will pass. Everything does in time, you know, and remember, I'm always here, if you want me."

Lalage and Madge were as close as they had been before their visit to Foxcove, but neither to Madge, nor to Ann, could Lalage talk of what kept her awake at night and tormented her by day. Now and then, of course, she slept, but she wished she hadn't had to, for then she wouldn't have seen Conan's face, nor the coldness of Delorme as he had left her.

"I am going to Florence," he had said, as they sat in her drawing-room. "I don't know how long I shall be there; perhaps three months, perhaps longer."

She had ached inside as she drank in every line of his face

which had now become so important to her, longing to touch him, but knowing she had forfeited that right. She wasn't quite certain when she realised she had fallen in love with him, nor did it seem strange to her that she could do so, and still think of Conan. They had separate places in her heart: Conan was of the past, Gaston the present.

" Will you . . . that is . . . will you be coming back to England?"

His eyes, which had once held nothing but amusement, and warm affection, had been empty, as if he had had no more to give her.

" I don't know. It is possible; one day."

" Yes, of course."

She hadn't known what to say to him. She had wanted to tell him of the awful suspicions she had had of him, and to beg his forgiveness. Once, she could have opened her soul to Gaston, but she had had no words for the stranger who had risen to bid her a formal good-bye.

She had wished him bon voyage, knowing that she sounded like a small girl, politely wishing one of her mother's friends a happy holiday, whilst Gaston had kissed her hand very conventionally, and had gone on his way.

The long winter passed, and then came Spring, but the sunshine and the sight of daffodils in the park didn't lighten Lalage's misery. Then, one day in March, she went into the morning-room to write her letters. She wrote many letters nowadays, for it filled up time, and reading the answers took up even more of the empty spaces in her life.

She caught sight of herself in the mirror, pausing to consider the image, as if it were someone else. It was a beautiful face. She had no conceit, but neither was she blind. The eyes were sad, the cheeks a trifle thinner. Fine-drawn and rather pale, but the loveliness was in no way diminished, and she was glad, although Gaston wasn't there to see it, and probably never would see it again.

When Orchard, her parlourmaid, came to tell her that she

had a visitor, she was not surprised. She had grown used to
an unending stream of callers, encouraging them, to keep
herself from being alone with her thoughts. She nodded. More
chit-chat over the coffee cups, with a pinch of spicy scandal
thrown in, but it would pass another hour.

"Who is it? Mrs. Deauville? She said she might call to-
day."

"No, Miss Lalage, it's M. Gaston."

The parlourmaid had never managed to announce the comte
properly, but this time Lalage scarcely noticed it. She felt
weak, as if she had been ill for a long time as she told the
girl to shew him in, and when he crossed the room, she could
hardly get up to greet him. The mere sight of him had drained
all her strength away.

He touched her fingers with his lips, not bothering with small
talk.

"Well, *ma petite*? You are better?"

"Yes, thank you." The polite child, on her best behaviour.
"Much better."

"He has gone? He no longer haunts you?"

Suddenly the small girl vanished for good, and Lalage was a
woman again, needing him desperately, completely honest, as
she knew she had to be.

"I think of him now and then. Occasionally, I dream of
him."

He looked at her soberly.

"We cannot live with a spectre between us. You must tell
me the real truth, and you know that I shan't blame you for it.
Were you in love with him?"

She raised her shoulders helplessly.

"I honestly don't know: I can't be sure."

All at once she found she was gripping Delorme's hand very
tightly.

"Tuesday gave me things which . . ."

"I know, I know, but it was more than that, wasn't it?
Don't be afraid. These things happen."

"Yes, I think it may have been more than that." She didn't know how to tell him what the first sight of Amberstone and Kilmartin had done to her. She didn't think she would ever be able to tell him; it was a matter which even Gaston couldn't share with her. "But whatever it was, it was over now."

"You are certain? I can wait, you know."

Her eyes filled with tears.

"But I can't. Oh, Gaston, I was so afraid that you wouldn't come back. I have had the most dreadful seven months of my life because I thought I'd lost you, and I do want you so."

He gave a quiet laugh, holding her against him, comforting her.

"Dearest, you could never lose me, but I had to give you time to heal from whatever had hurt you so."

He let her cry for a while, drawing her down on the sofa beside him. He didn't think that she had told him the whole truth, but perhaps she did not really know what the whole truth was. Angry though he had been when he had believed her to be Kilmartin's mistress and party to evil-doing, he had felt a strangeness about their relationship. He had never been able to put his finger on what it was, but instinct told him that it had been no ordinary *affaire*. Even when he had discovered that nothing had taken place between Lalage and Conan, his sense of disturbance had not lessened. They might not have been lovers, but there had been something very strong between them.

"I'm sorry." Lalage sat up, giving him a watery smile. "What must you think of me?"

"What I have always thought of you. You are breathtaking, even when you cry. Few women can manage that. Will you weep at our wedding?"

"Probably." She laughed a little at that. "Does that mean that you are going to ask me to marry you? Oh, I do hope you are, for I shall die if you don't."

"Then to avoid such a calamity, I had better do so, if you are sure that you are ready."

They were silent for a long while, holding each other's hands, their eyes locked. The image of Conan's face was fading from Lalage's mind, his last whisper almost forgotten.

Finally, she said:

" I'm ready, dearest."

" I too."

He hoped that her demons were really gone, but in every life some chances had to be taken. Conan Kilmartin was dead, whilst he and Lalage were young and alive, and he was deeply in love with her. He hoped that love would be strong enough, if ever the phantoms returned.

" So be it," he said, and pulled her back into his arms, holding her tightly as if he would never let her go. " Will you be my wife?"

" Yes."

She was smiling as he bent his head to kiss her.

" Oh, yes, Gaston, oh yes I will."

*　　　*　　　*

A month later, Lalage and Madge were in the middle of packing. The wedding was to be in Paris in three weeks time, and, as Madge had said more than once, Lalage seemed to have bought up half London to furnish her trousseau.

" Oh, by the way, a letter came for you." Madge fished in her apron pocket and handed the long white envelope to Lalage. " Looks like Miss Prue's writing."

" It is."

Lalage sat down at once to read it, scanning the lines quickly.

" Well, how is she, and the boy?"

" Fine, Prue has put on twelve pounds, she says, and Denzil is gaining weight every week too."

She paused, her brows coming together.

" What is it?"

Madge was sharp, acutely sensitive nowadays to the mere hint of trouble.

"Nothing, it's just the way Prue has worded the letter. It isn't important."

"Yes it is. We've had enough of secrets, you and I. Now, what does she say? I'll give you no peace until you tell me."

"Bully." Lalage's laugh was uncertain, looking down at the letter again. "Well, she says that Denzil is not a bit like her, or . . . or Conan either. She calls him her little changeling."

They exchanged a worried look.

"She also says that Jonus adores the baby. Although he's such a great lumbering creature, it seems that he's as gentle as a kitten with the child. So good-tempered too, it appears, and never barks or growls."

After a moment or two, Madge said:

"Hadn't meant to tell you this, but since I've said there are to be no more secrets between us, I must keep my part of the bargain. When we took Miss Prue back to Amberstone, just before we left for London, I had to go up to the attics to find young Gussie. Always missing when you wanted them, those girls were. Anyway, I found myself in that north wing again, though I didn't mean to go there. Lost my way, I suppose. Quite creepy, it felt, although I told myself not to be such a ninny."

Madge looked old.

"Yes, go on."

Lalage kept calm, but it was an effort.

"I could have sworn that I heard that noise again."

This time the look they exchanged was longer, fear beneath it.

"Jonus, probably. It must have been him. I expect he got shut up by mistake. He hates that."

"No, he was down in the kitchen. I'd just left him with a bone, and when I got back, he was still there, happy as a sandboy."

"Did you . . . did you look to see what it was?"

"Not likely!" Madge was emphatic. "What I did do the next day, though, was to go to the village to see the parson. He said, as a man of God, he couldn't accept the business of the curse, but it was true that some fifty years ago, a child was born at Amberstone that no one ever saw. Second son came along, eighteen months later, and he inherited. Rumour was that the first bairn had died, but nobody really believed it. Parson said he remembered his father talking about it. None of the servants ever went near that north wing, except for one old woman who'd been with the family for years. Then a new lass came, and she was a bold one. Nothing for it but she must go up there." Madge paused, looking down at her hands. " Seems she was white as a sheet when she got back to the others. Said there was something up there which snarled and scrabbled at the door as if it had long claws. She packed her bags and went the next morning, but none of the servants disbelieved her. They all knew, right enough."

She shrugged off her anxiety.

" Well, that's it. I expect it was just my fancy. Let's forget all about it, shall we. All's well with Miss Prue now, and I must go and ask John to get another trunk from the attics. And for goodness sake don't go shopping again this morning. You've got enough here to get married three times over."

Lalage got up slowly, taking a chemise and folding it mechanically, her thoughts a long way off. She had made a vow never to think of any part of her visit to Foxcove again, but Prue's letter, and Madge's tale, made the whole thing flood back into her mind, as fresh as ever.

She was remembering the look which had passed between Gaston and Conan, when the former said that he had taken Denzil. Kilmartin hadn't been thankful: he had been in a state of total shock. For a second or two he had been completely stunned, as if he knew that what Gaston was saying couldn't possibly be true. It had taken a real effort on his part to pull himself together, and accept Gaston's claim.

The chemise was put in a trunk, nervous fingers busy with a petticoat.

Gaston could very easily have produced a foundling; it wouldn't have been in the least difficult. There were many orphans needing homes, and baby-farms were an ugly blot on the face of respectable society.

Prue had said the child didn't look like her, or like Conan, and that she called him a changeling. Perhaps she was nearer to the truth than she realised.

But, if Gaston had not lied, and Denzil really was Conan's son, albeit not favouring either of his parents; if the baby had been kept tucked away in some other part of the house, and if Jonus was as tame as he appeared to be, there still remained one fearful question to be answered.

What had been locked up in that tiny, remote attic? What manner of creature was it, and, worse, could it possibly still be there?